'Can you ho
place?' she a
the end on his

As he reached up to take it his fingers brushed hers, and he felt a tremor he suspected was as much hers as his. He took the quivering fingers in his hand and lifted them to his lips, pressing a kiss into the soft palm of her hand.

'You've been wonderful,' he said, releasing her hand as she tried to tug it free. 'Here you are, calmly bandaging me up, when most women would be having hysterics or at the very least weeping copiously.'

'You don't have a very high opinion of women, do you?' she remarked, reaching around his body with the length of material.

He could feel the softness of her breasts against his back, and smell the fragrance of her hair as it brushed against his face. It made him think things he shouldn't think—especially about a colleague who was treating him.

Dear Reader

Doctors in the Outback, this series of four books set in the Australian Outback, of which OUTBACK MARRIAGE is the second, was prompted by a big change in my own life. My husband and I shifted from a house on the very edge of Australia, overlooking a broad stretch of water that feeds in from the Pacific Ocean, to a small cottage in a small Outback town (population about 2,500) in Central Queensland. From the beach to the bush—that's an Aussie word for anywhere that isn't in a city.

After the rush and bustle of the tourist-oriented city where we lived before, the relaxed pace of the Outback really suits us. Where before we had jet-skis roaring past as we ate breakfast on the front deck, now we have a large and very quiet kangaroo occasionally popping in to feed on our well-watered back lawn, and the most dominant noise is birdsong.

I am really enjoying my new life in the Outback, and I hope these books will bring you a taste of it—a taste of the variety of life in the bush, the highs and lows, the tears and laughter, and, of course, the love those that live out here seek and find.

With best wishes

Meredith Webber

OUTBACK MARRIAGE

BY
MEREDITH WEBBER

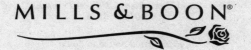

All the characters in this book have no existence outside the imagination of the author, and have no relation whatsoever to anyone bearing the same name or names. They are not even distantly inspired by any individual known or unknown to the author, and all the incidents are pure invention.

First published in Great Britain 2003
Harlequin Mills & Boon Limited,
Eton House, 18-24 Paradise Road, Richmond, Surrey TW9 1SR

© Meredith Webber 2003

ISBN 0 263 83871 4

Set in Times Roman 10½ on 11½ pt.
03-0104-50376

Printed and bound in Spain
by Litografia Rosés, S.A., Barcelona

CHAPTER ONE

BLYTHE knew, from the sidelong glances and puzzled frown, exactly what he'd been thinking so when the man-mountain with whom she'd been partnered finally asked the question, a hissed 'Are you really Lileth's sister?' she was ready with a sardonic 'Do I *look* like Lileth's sister?'

She nodded towards where the small, dainty, dark-haired and olive-skinned bride was seated at the table inside the chapel's tiny office. The space was so limited only the bride and groom, and the bishop flown in to perform the ceremony, would fit, so Blythe, acting-bridesmaid, and the best man, whom no one had bothered to introduce, were standing outside the rear door, awaiting the call to witness the happy couple's signatures.

The sun pressed down on them, adding to the heat the man's scrutiny was causing. Though admittedly she'd drawn his attention to the difference between her and her stepsister—had virtually invited him to look!

And look he did—his intent grey gaze travelling slowly over her body, hesitating where her breasts were squeezed into the too-small dress, no doubt noticing the unfashionable curves the clinging material accentuated.

She contemplated slapping his hard-planed, suntanned, arrogantly handsome face and decided her mother was already under enough stress without adding to it by making a scene at this stage of the proceedings.

'Not much!' he drawled—eventually—and she rolled her eyes and thought unkind things about whether heat affected the working of these western men's brains, or if it was life among the cattle made them so slow.

Here she was, five-ten and blonde and definitely not a size ten, positively squeezed into a bridesmaid's dress intended for her other—smaller—stepsister and he'd just figured out he had the wrong partner. Afraid she'd pop a seam, she edged gingerly into the inch of shade—all the midday sun was offering—beside the wall.

Any minute now sweat would start oozing from her body, leaving unattractive damp patches on the aqua stretch satin of the dress.

How could a couple of signatures take so long?

Or was the bishop giving the newlyweds a pep talk?

'You're blonde, for one thing.'

'Staggering powers of observation!' Blythe muttered at her companion, as the sun sucked out any last vestige of politeness she might have retained under the trying circumstances.

'Slow!' the man remarked, nodding to show he'd understood her rudeness. 'Actually, I'm surprised I'm functioning at all. I didn't arrive until late last night, then was hijacked into a party. Some of the lads who work here decided Mark needed a bachelor party and, though he trotted off to bed at a reasonable hour, the hands seem to feel I should stay. I think I managed a few hours' sleep although they seem to have made things worse, not better.'

He was rubbing his forehead as he spoke and, pitiful though he looked, this massive country bumpkin, Blythe steeled herself against offering any sympathy. In fact, she was feeling bitchy enough to do the opposite.

'Self-inflicted pain—serves you right!'

The glare he shot her way would have shrivelled a lesser mortal, but she'd been glared at by experts in her life, so ignored it.

Although the eyes that delivered it were arresting, now she looked a bit closer. Grey, definitely, but with a darker line around the outsides of the irises, complementing night-dark lashes and eyebrows.

'I am not hungover.' He stated the words with a grimness that suggested he might have felt better had he been. 'Merely tired.'

Blythe ignored the protest and continued her assessment. His hair was the same heavy black, cut ruthlessly short—no doubt in honour of the big event.

'Witnesses, please.'

The bishop called to them, then stepped aside to let them in, but the big man took up all the room, so in the end the bride and groom had to be evicted while Blythe and...she peered across to where his name was printed on the official document—Callum Whitworth—heavens! He was one of *them,* one of the cattle kings!...signed their names.

Then it was done, and the string quartet, imported to the cattle property at great expense by Lileth's grandfather, swung into some approximation of a triumphant wedding march. The bishop led the bride and groom back into the church and down the aisle with the attendants moving decorously behind.

'I always feel the triumph is overdone at this stage,' Blythe's partner whispered. 'I mean, who's won?'

'True love, of course!' Blythe whispered back, allowing only a little sarcasm to leak into the words. 'I thought you country lads were romantics, not cynics!'

'Once bitten, twice shy!' he growled as flash bulbs popped and handfuls of rose petals were flung at the radiant bride.

Friends and relatives crowded around, pushing Blythe and her partner aside, though the man had the good manners to take her arm when a particularly insistent matron in flowered dress and matching hat shoved against her in an effort to get a picture.

'So who are you?' he asked, in a voice that told her he

couldn't give a damn but understood being polite to her was part of his duties for the day.

'I'm Lileth's stepsister. Not included in the wedding party on account of not fitting the size requirements, but a last-minute replacement when Mary-Lynne developed mumps.'

Halfway through delivering this succinct explanation, another thought struck Blythe.

'If you're a Whitworth, you're a relative. You must have known I wasn't Mary-Lynne.'

Her comment surprised a smile into life on his face, and for a moment she wondered if she'd have to rethink her opinion of cowboys. The man was devilishly handsome when he smiled—heart-stoppingly so!

'No one in the family's seen much of the girls since they were little,' he said, the smile disappearing and a faint frown returning. 'I think when their mother died and their father decided he was better qualified to raise them than the string of governesses and maids my grandfather wanted to provide, they were not cut off so much as set beyond the pale.'

'And, of course, once their father had the bad taste to marry my mother, they went further out of favour.' Blythe found her cynicism matching his with ease.

'Which is your mother?' he asked, peering across to where a clutch of women pressed around the bride.

'The one with the sway back from bending over backwards to make sure she treated her stepdaughters just as well as she treated her own daughter.'

The grey eyes studied her more sharply, something in the regard making Blythe regret her silly flippancy.

'That sounded worse than I meant it to be.' She rushed to make amends. 'My mother is actually the sweetest, kindest woman imaginable and would do anything for anyone. She's also genuinely in love with Brian and unstinting in her love for all three of her daughters, step or not!'

'You don't sound exactly happy about having this paragon for a mother,' Callum Whitworth remarked.

Blythe grinned at him.

'Makes it very hard to say no when she asks a favour of you. Look at me. For a start I was meant to leave for the UK two weeks ago, but Lileth's whirlwind romance, her decision to get married, meant I had to delay my departure and give up the job I'd arranged to take on there. Then her grandfather steps in and insists she wed on the family's kingdom, and I have to fly up here to the back of beyond, spending money I can ill afford. And what happens within minutes of my arrival late yesterday, but Mary-Lynne swells up. Mum does her "please, Blythe" thing again, and I'm squeezed into a dress two sizes too small and made look like an absolute gig as part of the wedding party.'

'Why did it cost you money to fly up?'

Of all her complaints, it was the last bit she'd expected him to pick up on.

'It's a long way from Brisbane to the Northern Territory. You may not realise it, but this place is actually a long way from anywhere. I had to fly to Darwin, then get another plane to—'

'But my grandfather arranged to fly in all the wedding guests.' He cut into her catalogue of complaints. 'One flight from Brisbane and another from Sydney.'

'Yes, well…' Blythe said, and looked around for distraction. It was hard to explain that she didn't want to be beholden to a man to whom she wasn't related. It was something even her mother hadn't understood.

'Seems we're wanted.' Before she had to put this reluctance into words, the man took her arm and steered her towards the newly married couple. 'Photo call!'

They posed for group photos with the parents of both bride and groom, then the photographer ushered them into a golf buggy and, with one of the property's workmen driving, they followed another buggy containing bride, groom and photographer along a carefully smoothed track.

'Photos by the lagoon are a tradition at Mount Spec,' Blythe's companion remarked, his voice as dry as the hot air stirred to a feeble breeze by their progress.

'Been there and done that, have you?' Blythe guessed, and the man smiled again.

'Been there and done that!' he agreed.

'You don't sound as if marriage has brought you a lot of joy!' Blythe remarked, and heard confirmation of her guess in the harshness of his laugh.

'It's worked better for my brother,' was all he said, because by now they'd reached the banks of the placid, tree-shaded lagoon, its waters strewn with Lileth's name flowers—blue, pink and white waterlilies.

'It *is* lovely,' Blythe found herself admitting.

'Come on, don't turn sentimental on me,' Callum complained. 'Your caustic tongue's just about made things bearable because I find myself wondering who you're going to knife next! If you're about to become increasingly mawkish and womanly as the day progresses, I may as well drown myself now and be done with it.'

Blythe opened her mouth to retaliate, then closed it again when she couldn't decide which bit of his insult to protest at first. In the end she settled on what was probably the weakest point of all, firing a look of loathing at him as she straightened to her full height and expanded her chest.

'I do *happen* to *be* a woman!' she snorted, then heard the sound of fabric tearing as the chest-expansion exercise proved a disastrous mistake.

'Oh, sh—'

Firm fingers closed over her lips, cutting off the word she'd intended saying.

'Not in front of the bishop,' Callum said, the grey eyes dancing with delight at her predicament.

Blythe pressed her arm against the seam that was giving way and glanced frantically around.

'The bishop's not here and it's not funny!' She scowled at her companion in case her whispered retort didn't carry enough aggravation. 'Hell's bells, what do I do now?'

She was clutching the top of the strapless dress with one hand and trying to hide the split with the other when Lileth approached.

'What have you done now?' she demanded, and Blythe, though used to her younger step-sibling's uncanny ability to sniff out problems, was staggered to find it working so well on her wedding day.

'Split the damn dress!' she admitted. 'I told Mum this was likely to happen.'

If anything, Lileth looked relieved. Of course, relief wasn't enough to stop her bringing up the list of disasters Blythe had already caused, including Mary-Lynne's mumps and Blythe's failure to be the right size for the aesthetic balance of the wedding party, but in the end she mellowed.

'I suppose the dress thing isn't so bad,' she finally declared. 'Mark and I had already decided we wanted more photos of just the two of us. I mean, if Mary-Lynne had been here, it would have been different, but Callum's only best man because he works with Mark...'

Blythe glanced at the maligned attendant to see how he was taking his cousin's blunt assessment of his friendship with the groom.

He seemed remarkably unfazed, even going so far as to wink at Blythe, as if to assure her he was OK with the put-down.

'You're a funny lot, you Whitworths,' she remarked, when Lileth had gone to reclaim her groom and one hundred per cent of the photographer's attention.

'Be grateful we are,' Callum told her. 'Now, where are you staying? At the main house or in one of the bungalows? As we've been officially dismissed, we can go back and you can change.'

To Cal, it seemed an eminently sensible suggestion, but the look of dismay in the brown eyes of the stand in told him she didn't see it in the same light.

'More problems?'

'Not of my own making,' she hastened to point out, a reassuringly waspish tone back in her voice. 'Any more than Mary-Lynne throwing out a swelling or two was my fault.'

She hesitated, then added almost in an undertone, 'Not that anyone's likely to believe *that*!'

Cal found himself chuckling.

'What are you? Some harbinger of doom?'

Blythe nodded, the movement shifting the abundance of wavy fair hair so golden light shot through it.

'I'm known in the family for being a walking disaster area—an accident looking for somewhere to happen. It got that way I was paranoid about stepping on cracks in the pavement, thinking I must be doing something wrong to be causing so much trouble. While as for cats, black, brown or brindle, I steer clear of them as well.'

Cal laughed again—she had to be joking—though she didn't smile. In fact, for someone in a wedding party, she looked particularly gloomy.

The gloomy expression failed to diminish the attractiveness of the face framed by the fair hair, and he found himself waiting for her to smile—guessing the effect would be pleasant.

Though why *he* was laughing, he didn't know. Fate had

embroiled him in this 'happy families' reunion, but nothing was going to make him like it. They'd walked as far as the buggy but the reluctance he was feeling stopped him climbing in.

His companion, in spite of a dress that was slipping lower by the minute, and incidentally revealing a better and better view of full, rich, creamy breasts, seemed even less eager to return to the homestead.

'I haven't any clothes to change into.'

The blunt statement drew his attention back to the woman.

'None?'

'Well, I've the jeans and shirt I wore to come up but, having glimpsed, as we scampered down the aisle, the outfits other women are wearing, I think changing into jeans and a T-shirt, which says ''I suffer from occasional feelings of adequacy'' could well send the bride into hysterics.'

Cal nodded. From the little he knew of Lileth, the ersatz bridesmaid was probably right. And though his mind was having trouble with the notion of a woman arriving at a wedding—or anywhere for that matter—without several suitcases packed with clothes, the T-shirt intrigued him.

'Do you?' he asked.

She looked at him, the luminous brown eyes puzzled.

'Do I what?

'Suffer from occasional feelings of adequacy?'

The smile lit up her eyes and seemed to produce a kind of radiance beneath her clear, creamy skin.

'Only very occasionally,' she told him, her tone suggesting it was a secret she was sharing just with him.

Was it the implied intimacy, or the smile—perhaps the radiance? Cal didn't know, but he found his body reacting in a way it hadn't for a long, long time.

Oh, no!

Definitely not!

He brought it under control with the question he should have asked.

'You came to wedding without any spare clothes? What were you going to wear if you didn't end up as bridesmaid?'

'I didn't set out without any clothes,' she told him, her voice weary with the acceptance of bad luck. 'They just missed the mail plane out of Darwin. Actually, they didn't so much miss the mail plane as were put on the wrong one. I came to Mount Spec and they went to Tokyo.'

Cal suspected laughter would be the wrong reaction, so he shook his head while trying to control it, but in the end he lost the battle and the light-hearted chuckle grew until he found himself laughing more heartily than he had for months.

Since, in fact, his long-lost cousin had arrived in Creamunna on a 'find her family' mission and proceeded to fall in love with his boss.

Not that Mark hadn't reciprocated the love thing—poor fool that he was.

'When you've quite finished enjoying yourself at my expense, perhaps we could return to the homestead. I'm in the shearers' quarters but Mum's in a bungalow that has curtains. Perhaps I can do a sarong type thing with one of them.'

The snappy tone stopped his laughter, although the idea of someone wearing a curtain to a wedding threatened to start it again.

'Mum always has a packet of safety pins in her luggage so you can help me fix it,' the unusual bridesmaid continued, as if this was a perfectly normal conversation.

He stared at the woman, unable to believe she was serious. First about the curtain, and secondly about him helping her.

The dark eyes flashed fire, daring him to refuse.

'After all,' she said, 'it was your fault in the first place. If you hadn't been so rude, I wouldn't have had to breathe in…'

Cal shook his head. Perhaps he *had* had too much to drink the previous night, though he could swear all he'd touched was light beer.

Maybe someone had spiked it.

That would explain this increasingly bizarre scenario.

Though the woman was real enough, sitting there in the beribboned golf buggy, clutching her dress in one hand and impatiently beckoning him to get on board with the other.

'We don't have all day,' she told him. 'I mean, how many photos can they possibly want?'

He got in and directed the young driver to take them back to the homestead.

'The little blue bungalow, in fact,' his companion corrected, then she turned to Cal and put out her free hand. 'By the way, I'm Blythe Jones. If you're going to be wrapping me up, the least I can do is introduce myself.'

Cal shook the hand, and introduced himself with a brief 'Cal Whitworth'.

He should have added, And I have no intention of being part of the wrapping process, but he suspected she'd ignore him.

They reached the neatly laid-out settlement that was the heart and soul of the Whitworth cattle empire. The huge old homestead set in lush, borehole-watered gardens dominated the cluster of outbuildings and sheds, while the bungalows gathered around the perimeter fence like chicks around a hen.

'Good! It's out of sight of the marquee so no one will notice one of the curtains coming down,' Blythe said, hopping out of the buggy and reaching back to grab his arm.

'We'll have to hurry. We don't want to attract attention by being late.'

'More attention than wearing a curtain will attract?' Cal muttered at her, but he allowed himself to be dragged inside.

'There—the green one. The colour's not good but the material looks soft and reasonably drapable. Can you get it down and remove any hooks from the top? Or should I just cut the top off? That might be better. Get it down and we'll have a look.'

Cal had a very good idea of what Grace, his ex-wife and current chatelaine of Mount Spec, would have to say about guests cutting up the curtains.

'Couldn't you borrow a dress?'

The bridesmaid sent him a look that suggested he was, in her opinion, down in the bottom percentile in the IQ lists.

'I've already split the dress I borrowed. I am two sizes larger than anyone in my family, and probably at least one size larger than anyone at the wedding. Now, are you going to get it down, or shall I?'

Too bemused to argue further, he pulled a chair over to the window and climbed on it. The woman had disappeared, presumably in search of safety pins and scissors.

And Grace was far too obsessed with possessions anyway!

He allowed himself a small chuckle as he unhooked the curtain.

'Certainly a cutting job,' he said, hearing footsteps behind him.

He turned to find his bridesmaid wrapped in a towel, revealing not only the tops of the soft creamy breasts but considerable length of fine, shapely legs.

'Just pull the other curtains across so you don't notice it's missing,' the legs' owner ordered. 'If Mum happens to come back here before the reception, I don't want her freaking out.'

He rearranged the remaining material and climbed carefully off the stool, proffering the curtain.

'I can't cut and hold the towel up,' she informed him, passing him the scissors but lifting the bottom of the curtain and weighing it experimentally in her free hand.

With only a slight qualm, he hacked the top folded part off the curtain.

'Great!' Blythe told him. 'Now give it to me. I'll duck into the bathroom and see what I can do, while you stand by with pins.'

She handed him a packet of safety pins, took the curtain and disappeared again, but a howl of frustration suggested things weren't going too well.

'You'll have to help,' she said, storming back out, this time wrapped in shiny green curtain rather than the towel. 'See, I can get this round here but it keeps slipping down and I'll end up falling out into the ice cream. This one-shouldered sarong style is all the fashion, so if you could pin this bit around here...'

She twisted to show him where and the slippery material slid downward, revealing more of the full breasts—even a shadow of pink aureole.

'Y-you're not wearing a b-bra!' he stammered, his eyes drawn inexorably to the beautiful sight.

'Of course I'm not wearing a bra.' She hitched the material back up before he had time for more than a quick glimpse. 'Bras one wears under T-shirts have straps—you can't wear one with a strapless dress. Just pretend you're a doctor examining a patient and get on with it.'

He got on with it, an exercise which involved having to slide his fingers inside the wrappings so they pressed against the yielding flesh. And try as he may to think like a doctor, his fingers had never trembled when examining a patient, and other bits of his anatomy *never* showed an interest in patients.

'Actually, it doesn't look too bad,' he admitted ten minutes later when Blythe pronounced herself satisfied with the result. 'The colour suits you.'

She'd fluffed her hair around her shoulders with her fingers, producing a carelessly sexy look, and 'doesn't look too bad' was an understatement. But she seemed unaware of the effect, simply studying the finished result in the mirror for a moment before walking—carefully—away.

'Just as well I'm not a pink person or I'd have had to nick one of the living room drapes from the homestead.'

She grinned at him and he found himself smiling back.

'Shall we?' he said, offering her his arm.

'I guess so,' she replied, slipping her hand into the crook of his elbow, although something in her voice told him she wasn't nearly as certain about this escapade as she made out.

But as they walked through the garden, dread at the prospect of spending the rest of the afternoon playing 'happy families' overwhelmed all other concerns. He'd be flat out maintaining a polite façade himself, so the bridesmaid would have to fend for herself.

'Oh, did your luggage come?'

Grace was standing beside her grandfather-in-law, greeting the guests as they entered the marquee. She ignored Cal for the moment, but he saw the way she looked at Blythe and read a level of pique in her expression. Grace liked to outshine all opposition, and to have to compete with a tall, statuesque blonde, even one draped in a curtain, wouldn't sit well with her.

Cal felt better immediately.

Intrigued by the little byplay, he waited for Blythe's answer, but she managed to avoid answering, merely shaking hands with his grandfather and moving on into the room.

'Grace!' Cal acknowledged his ex-wife with a polite smile and a kiss on the cheek, then he, too, moved on, shaking his grandfather's hand, promising to catch up with the old man later, before following his partner further into the reception area.

It seemed to Cal that males of all ages were making a beeline for his curtain-clad partner, she obviously had a destination in mind for she swayed gracefully through the crowd until she came to a slim, upright woman standing quietly beside a tall, elegant man.

'Oh, you're here,' she said to Cal, after she'd greeted the couple with kisses and hugs. 'This is my mum, Lorice Bell, and Brian, my stepfather,' she explained.

'And not a sway back in sight,' Cal whispered in her ear as he stretched out a hand to greet the older couple. 'I'm Callum Whitworth.'

'Yes, I knew you were,' Lorice said. 'How do you do?'

The greeting was polite enough but her voice was distracted, and her eyes were focussed on her daughter.

'Did it split?' she asked with enough resignation to suggest to Cal she'd been expecting just such a disaster.

Blythe nodded, then began to talk about the ceremony, no doubt anxious to avert questions about the substitute garment. Brian Bell drew Cal aside, and seemed about to ask something when Chris arrived.

'Stood up well to the pressure, old man,' he said, clapping Cal on the back.

'Brian, you've met my brother Chris, have you?'

Brian nodded but Cal was more interested in Blythe's reaction. She was glancing from him to Chris, no doubt sizing up the similarities and differences. Though three years apart in age, they'd always been alike enough to have been twins so he'd seen people's surprise all his life.

'Where are the kids?' he asked Chris, but before Chris could reply, they arrived. Jenny, slim—too thin?—and elegant even at twelve, while Sam at thirteen was struggling with the onset of adolescence—a brash loudmouth one minute, an uncertain kid the next. He'd spent the morning with them, but they'd been dressed in their usual home clothes of shorts and T-shirts. Seeing them dressed up made him realise how quickly they were growing up.

'Hi, Dad! Good show!'

Blythe watched as the newly arrived youngsters greeted her partner-for-the-day. She was conscious of a spurt of disappointment when she heard the word 'Dad', then, forgetting the insecurity of her clothing, shrugged it off.

'Careful,' Callum whispered to her, before returning to a conversation with his children.

Blythe watched the interaction between the three, intrigued by Cal's intensity—as if he didn't have a lot of time to spend with them—and a look in his eyes that was a mix of sadness and regret.

Blythe hauled back her imagination before it got totally carried away. This man's life—and the time he spent with his children—was nothing to do with her, and his eyes might always look like that.

She looked around, distracting herself by trying to guess which of the women at the wedding was his wife. Surely she must be here. Why hadn't she come to lay claim to her husband?

And how come his brother Chris had greeted Callum as if this was the first time he'd seen him for a while? Perhaps he managed another property. But even if he didn't live here, surely he'd have been at the pre-wedding dinner the previous evening.

She tried to remember an earlier conversation—had he said he'd arrived late last night?

The man called Chris was saying something, but Blythe

missed it, too busy regretting her refusal to join the family at the same dinner where she might have been able to sort out who was who in the Whitworth dynasty.

But with nothing suitable to wear, grabbing a snack from the well-stocked kitchen in the shearers' quarters had seemed the best option, no matter how much her mother had protested.

'Come on, we're due on stage again.' Cal touched her arm and she realised the children had moved on and the guests were being gently herded towards tables.

He held her elbow to steer her through the crowd, then parked her behind a chair at the main table, at the top of a horseshoe-shaped arrangement of smaller tables.

'Who else is sitting here?' she asked, peering at the place-cards for a clue.

'Mark's parents beyond me, and on the other side the groom, then bride, then your parents, my grandfather and Grace.'

'The woman I met as I came in? Is she a later wife? She's very young.'

'She's thirty-five and his granddaughter-in-law,' Callum said, and added, 'Twice over.'

'Twice over?' Blythe turned to him as she repeated the cryptic remark, and saw a shadow of something she couldn't understand flicker in his eyes. Then he smiled, lips tilting more on one side than the other.

'Here comes the bride,' he whispered, sidestepping her question.

The quartet, now installed in a corner of the marquee, began to play, and a hush descended as the gathering awaited Mark's and Lileth's entrance. They made their way through an aisle of clapping and cheering guests, finally reaching the table.

'I won't ask where it came from,' Lileth whispered to Blythe, 'but thanks.'

Rendered speechless by the expression of gratitude, Blythe took her place, sinking into the chair Cal held for her.

CHAPTER TWO

AS THE guests took their seats, waiters attended the main table, offering a choice of wines and non-alcoholic drinks.

'Champagne! We'll all have champagne!' Lileth announced to the others at the main table.

'I'll have mineral water,' Blythe murmured to the waiter, 'but if you'd pour it into my champagne glass I'd be grateful.'

'Cheating?' Callum asked.

She flashed a smile at him, but she noticed he'd also had his glass filled with water.

'I'm thinking of the pins,' she told him in an undertone. 'As long as Lileth thinks I'm having a drink she won't make a fuss, and as long as I don't have a drink I should be able to get myself out of this garment later and not have to call on you to unpin me!'

The arrested look in his grey eyes sent a flutter of apprehension down Blythe's spine.

You can *not* be attracted to a married man, she reminded herself.

Out loud—and for safety's sake—she asked, 'Where's your wife?'

'I don't have one,' he said calmly, then he lifted his hand to acknowledge his daughter's wave.

Blythe considered this statement and amended her silent command.

You can *not* be attracted to a man you'll probably never see again. She sought refuge in flippancy.

'Just children? Are there more than two? Do you have them scattered across the countryside?'

'Well, I'm glad to see you've recovered your acidity!' he remarked. 'For a while there I thought the evening was going to degenerate into polite exchanges of bland social niceties.'

Ouch! Blythe thought, sneaking another look at the man to whom she had no intention of being attracted.

'I can do social niceties as well as the next person,' she informed him, then rather spoilt the lofty remark by adding, 'When I so desire!'

He laughed—splintering the air between them with the rich melodious sound.

Distracted from his bride by the laughter, Mark turned to Blythe.

'That must have been some joke,' he said, his blue eyes warm and friendly. 'Haven't heard Cal laugh like that the whole year he's been in Creamunna.'

'But—'

Blythe began to protest that it wasn't a joke, then frowned as several remarks and assumptions bumped together in her head, presenting her with pieces of a puzzle that certainly didn't fit together.

'You...' she began, then realised she'd lost Mark's attention once again, so she turned to Cal.

'Lileth said something earlier about you working with Mark, and he says you've been together a year. Together doing what? Mark's a doctor!'

The smile that tilted one side of his lips more than the other put in a fugitive appearance.

'And I couldn't possibly be? Too slow? Not enough neurones to synapse effectively?'

'No doubt you have your full compliment of neurones,' Blythe said sniffily. 'But you're a Whitworth—land barons, cattle kings, all that stuff! Why work your butt off being a doctor?'

This time the smile held a touch of steel. 'Land barons

and cattle kings also work their butts off, and under far worse conditions than most doctors.'

'Not when they're on twelve-hour shifts in A and E,' she challenged. 'A bit of dust and heat can't compare with the blood and anguish.'

'Cynical *and* argumentative!' he responded, but Cal's eyes were studying her intently, as if trying to figure something out. 'And what makes you an expert in the conditions in A and E?'

'Been there and done that!' Blythe told him, echoing the phrase he'd used earlier.

'Been a doctor?'

She grinned at him.

'Now who's being incredulous? Why shouldn't I have been a doctor? In fact, it's present tense, not past. I still am a doctor, if temporarily unemployed.'

'Because of the wedding?'

Was there a hint of sympathy in his words? A gleam of fellow-feeling in his eyes?

'Because of the wedding.' She sighed. 'But don't think you've diverted me from the original conversation. I didn't have a long line of cattlemen behind me—or, in fact, a long line of anything much—so becoming a doctor seemed as good a choice as any other. But for you—are you the younger son? Did you miss the direct line of inheritance by sheer bad luck so were sent off into the world to fend for yourself?'

He didn't answer immediately, and she couldn't tell if he was waiting until the waiter had set their first course in front of them and moved on, or was thinking up some story to tell her.

Cal looked at the plate of food and wondered what it was. He was also wondering how to answer Blythe's question. Or whether to answer it at all, considering she was only asking out of politeness and they'd never see each other again after today.

A momentary flash of something resembling regret took him by surprise, until he realised it must have been caused by the fact that his body found her attractive—and possibly the lack of action the same body had been getting lately!

'I think it's a terrine of some description,' she said, apparently picking up on his first problem. 'Mine's seafood—no doubt as a nod to non-meat-eaters. Would you like to swap?'

'Why is yours different to mine?' he demanded, studying what looked like a very appetising concoction set in front of his partner.

'It's the thing at weddings these days,' she explained in the kindly voice of a kindergarten teacher. 'Alternate meals so if I don't fancy pork, I can swap it for your chicken.'

Cal was about to point out they had neither pork nor chicken when the MC rose and announced the bishop would now say grace.

'Just as well we were discussing the food rather than eating it,' Blythe whispered, putting his own relief into words. 'Do you want the seafood? I'm always a bit wary about anything aquatic when I'm this far from the sea.'

Was his face giving so much away that under cover of the grace she switched the plates?

The bishop resumed his seat, conversation restarted, and Blythe picked up a fork and attacked the food.

'I like terrines, though it's best not to think about what might have gone into them,' she said chattily. 'A variety of offal quite "offen".'

He chuckled at the weak joke, she grinned at him, and the twinge of regret he'd felt earlier turned to something stronger.

It's only because you know you won't be seeing her again that you're interested, he told himself. Has to be that, he assured himself, because you've never liked smart-mouthed women.

He ate his seafood arrangement, but his eyes kept straying to the expanse of bare skin across the smart-mouthed woman's—he decided on *chest* and shoulders, so pale in contrast to the vivid green of the makeshift dress.

'Is it slipping? Please, tell me it's not?'

The urgency of the whispered pleas brought his wayward gaze back under control but he felt his cheeks heat and hoped he hadn't reverted to the blushing problems he'd suffered in adolescence.

'No, no!' he said, pretending nonchalance, 'I was simply considering how overpriced most women's clothes must be if you can achieve such an effect with a few pins and a curtain.'

'But it was probably a very expensive curtain,' she reminded him, then, to add to his confusion, she smiled again. 'And the pins were gold-plated!'

Pins—pinning the material…

He scanned his scattered wits for a conversational topic that didn't keep reminding him of how soft her breasts had felt, or how white her skin was.

'I am the older son, as it happens,' he said, remembering her earlier assumption and grasping it with the desperation of a drowning man. 'Though the family holdings are in a company and we all have a share so there's no such thing as anyone missing out through an accident of birth order. Family members who work here are paid the same wages as non-family workers.'

'But you don't work here, you're a doctor,' she reminded him, leaning back in her chair so the waiter could take her empty plate.

And look down the front of the curtain dress, Cal thought with unaccustomed surliness.

He shifted in the hope it would spoil the view, but the young man had moved on.

And now Cal had forgotten what they'd been discussing before the waiter had arrived. He glanced at his companion and found the brown eyes looking so directly at him he realised she was expecting an answer to some question he'd lost for ever.

'What did you ask?'

'Are you sure you didn't have one too many last night?' She shook her head and added, 'I didn't ask a question—well, not recently—but you were explaining why you became a doctor.'

I was? Cal frowned. It wasn't something he usually talked about because—

The MC was on his feet again, this time to propose a loyal toast.

'I thought this kind of thing went out with Noah,' his partner grumbled, clutching her champagne glass and rising gingerly to her feet.

But she dutifully raised her glass, giving Cal the opportunity to check the pins were holding fast.

They sat again, and the waiters began circulating with larger plates.

'Considering where we are, I suppose it's a choice of beef or beef,' Blythe said, smiling with unnecessary warmth at their waiter.

'That looks more like chicken on your plate, but if you want beef I'd be happy to swap,' Cal said, pointing to her plate to divert her attention from the good-looking young man.

She glanced towards him and he could almost see the smart retort trembling on her lips, but something must have caught her attention for the brown eyes took on a puzzled look and she frowned at him as if trying to remember who he was.

'A bit of prawn caught between my teeth?' he asked, using his napkin to swipe hurriedly across his lips.

She shook her head, moving the mass of sexy hair, but the frown remained.

'Twice over! The old man's her grandfather-in-law twice over. And you're the older brother, not the oldest, so there are only two of you. Do you mean to tell me your wife married your brother?'

Blythe realised her disbelief must have been stridently expressed for Mark turned towards her and beyond Callum Mark's parents were also looking puzzled.

'Tell the entire gathering, why don't you!' Cal muttered, then he added, 'Not that most of them don't already know! You talk about *me* being slow. Don't your family talk to each other, that it's taken you this long to put it together? I'd have thought it was the kind of gossip Lileth would have been only too happy to pass on.'

Blythe flinched at the bite in his voice. No doubt the man had every reason to be bitter about such a situation, but that didn't give him the right to be sarcastic about *her* family.

'We usually have better things to discuss than gossip about other people's marriages.'

She gave him a fierce look, which would have worked better if he hadn't been so handsome and she didn't find him so attractive.

Rallying her defence mechanisms, she tried again. 'Besides, you've admitted you hardly know Lileth, so how can you possibly judge her like that?'

To her surprise he capitulated without argument, raising his hands to show he'd surrendered.

'Gross generalisation, I admit!' he said. 'I was put out because she breezed into town on her ''meet the family'' trip, and had barely said hello to me—the family she'd come to meet—when Mark swept her off her feet and they were planning a wedding. And though Mark hasn't said anything, I can't help feeling she'd be happier if he was working in the city so I fear I'm going to be left in the position he was in before I arrived—the only doctor in a town that really needs at least two.'

He sounded so depressed by this possibility Blythe would have liked to comfort him, but as she, too, had doubts about Lileth's ability to adapt to country life, in spite of her genetic heritage, she could hardly assure him it wasn't likely to happen.

The other topic she'd like to pursue was his wife's marriage to his brother but, having denied any interest in gossip, there was no way she could bring it up again—especially not under these circumstances.

Fortunately his attention had been diverted by Mark's mother, seated on his other side. It gave Blythe the opportunity to study him more closely.

And compare him to his brother, who was sitting at one of the lower tables, but well within viewing range. She could detect no visible reason for the errant wife preferring the younger son. In fact, the Whitworth next to her looked far more—not so much solid, but—manly?

Blythe eyed him again, searching for the right word, then realised Mark had said something to her and turned to answer him.

When Mark's attention was captured by Lileth, Blythe decided she'd be better off concentrating on her meal, not her companion. She pushed the chicken to one side and ate a small lettuce leaf.

'My mother had a book about social graces—advice on the right thing to do in any circumstance, the correct way to start or restart a conversation.'

The statement was so surprising Blythe turned to the companion she'd been determined to ignore, her raised fork arrested halfway to her lips.

'Are you implying I lack social graces?' she demanded.

Cal grinned as if amused by her pique.

'No, regretting I didn't read it.'

She found herself smiling back. 'Actually, I've read it—or listened to my mother's lectures, probably taken from the same source. Ask about your companion's occupation—well, I've kind of done that and you didn't seem too happy discussing it, given the uncertainty about Mark. Interests seem to be another innocuous topic. Shall I ask you about your interests?'

But before he could answer, another thought struck her.

'Your mother! You've a grandfather in common with Lileth and Mary-Lynne and I know he's running this particular show, but do your parents live here as well? Are they involved with the property?'

The look he gave her was more suspicious than anything else.

'I realise a high-minded family like yours doesn't gossip, but surely you must have had some interest in your stepsisters' history. In how the girls came to be motherless.'

Blythe closed her eyes and prayed to be sucked into a vortex or at the very least reduced to a blob of ectoplasm. Since neither outcome occurred, she opened them again and looked at Cal, seeking dark shadows of pain in his eyes but seeing only an implacable coldness.

'I'm sorry! The last few days have been so fraught I simply didn't think—let alone put two and two together. I *did* know the girls' mother had been killed while flying home from a brief visit to the property—along with her brother and his wife. Those were your parents? Were you and your brother brought up by the phalanx of maids and governesses you mentioned earlier?'

'We were much older and already in boarding school,' he said, then he turned his attention back to his meal, shifting his body in such a way Blythe felt he was shielding himself from further onslaughts of insensitivity.

She ate a little of her meal, but her appetite had deserted her. Turned to talk to Mark, but he was whispering to his bride. Finally, when the silence grew so taut she knew she had to break it or scream, she nudged Callum's arm, and murmured, 'My mother didn't tell me the bit in the book about how to cover gross faux pas, but if you'd just accept an apology and pretend to talk to me, people would stop looking at us and wondering what's going on.'

'I wouldn't have thought a little attention would bother you,' he said with the kind of smile designed to rile the receiver.

And rile it did, bringing to Blythe's mind all the frustrations and annoyances of the past twenty-four hours and fanning smouldering embers into a fierce conflagration.

'Well, it just so happens it doesn't,' she snapped. 'But why stop at furtive looks and murmurs when I can really attract attention? Here, hold this end of the curtain. I'll stand up on the table and unwind!'

He grasped her arm, looking so shocked by her threat she had to hide a smile.

'Y-you w-wouldn't!' he stuttered.

'Want to dare me?'

Cal studied her face, taking in the cocked eyebrow, the challenge in her eyes and a little flicker of a smile she'd allowed to flirt around her lips. And far from daring her, or even warning her of consequences should she do anything so rash, he found himself wanting to kiss her.

The idea of kissing someone as volatile as this shapely, caustic and erratic blonde was so shocking he wondered if he should take some time off when Mark returned from his honeymoon and go to the city for some rest and relaxation—or perhaps sin and sex would be a better way to put it.

If, of course, Mark did return from his honeymoon.

Gentle fingers rested lightly his hand.

'I wouldn't really do it, you know.'

The voice was equally gentle, but the 'wanting to kiss her' scenario was enough of a warning, so he wasn't going to be taken in by gentle voices.

'No?' Cal cocked an eyebrow of his own. 'From the little I've seen during our mercifully brief acquaintance, I find that hard to believe.'

The flicker of reaction he caught in her eyes told him his words had struck home, but he doubted he'd have hurt her. She probably practised that hurt look for use when the occasion warranted it.

'Well, I wouldn't—at least not here. Not and spoil Lileth's wedding. I do have some feelings for my family— though it's hard to remember that when they're throwing out swollen glands and forcing me into clothes two sizes too small.'

Hmm. She sounded contrite as well, but he wasn't going to fall for that either. Before he knew it, he'd be telling her things he hadn't spoken of for years.

'Dad!'

Jenny's voice saved him making a decision.

'There's a little kid at our table and he's really, really sick.'

The urgency in the words brought Cal immediately to his feet, and though Blythe began to rise, he rested his hand on her shoulder and eased her back down into her chair.

'Less obvious so less fuss if just one of the wedding party leaves the table,' he whispered, then crossed to the corner of the marquee where all the children had been seated at one big table.

The child's mother had apparently been alerted, for an anxious-looking woman knelt beside the little boy, her hands swiping ineffectually around his runny nose as the child gasped for breath. The tissues around his eyes were red and swollen, and red weals were coming up on his skin. There was no doubt the little fellow was suffering a severe, and potentially life-threatening allergic reaction to something.

A few guests were looking in that direction, but most were still focussed on either their meal or the wedding party at the top table.

'I'm a doctor,' Cal told the woman, scooping the child into his arms and heading for the nearest exit. 'Has this happened before? Do you know if he's allergic to anything?'

'Peanuts,' the woman, who was following Cal said. 'But he knows he's not allowed to eat them.'

'And he's what? Four? Five?'

'He's four and he did eat some peanuts.' Cal realised when Jenny replied that his daughter must be following them. 'There were some in a saucer on the table—the ones with the sweet red sugar coating, Dad.'

Outside the marquee, Cal moved with swift sure strides towards Mount Spec's clinic. Although small, it had a fully stocked dispensary and he knew there'd be adrenaline there. He held the little boy close, and felt the rapid heartbeat of tachycardia shaking the slight body.

As he approached the clinic, a middle-aged woman in a nurse's uniform came out onto the shady veranda.

'Trouble?'

'Anaphylactic shock—allergic reaction to peanuts. What dosages of epinephrine do you keep?'

The woman—she was new since he'd last visited so he didn't know her name—disappeared again, then returned with a couple of packages of drugs, holding them out in her hands so he could see the selection.

'We've Epi-pens as one of the stockmen is allergic to

bee stings, or prepacked injections of one in ten thousand adrenaline in point one mil doses or ampoules of one in one thousand.'

'We'll take an ampoule—draw up ten micrograms, and we can repeat it when necessary.'

Cal set the little boy down on a padded bench in the clinic's examination room, took the injection from the nurse and, after swabbing a patch of skin, slid the needle into the muscle, injecting the drug very slowly into the tissues.

'Will he be all right?'

Jen's question awoke Cal to the fact his daughter was still with them.

'Yes,' he said, dropping the empty syringe into a sharps container and turning to give his daughter a comforting hug. She'd responded well when she'd realised the child was sick but she was shaky now the emergency was over. 'I'll stay here a little longer and give him another injection if he needs it, but you can see he's already breathing more easily.'

The little boy still looked ill, but he was quiet, almost asleep and definitely not fighting for every breath.

The nurse had checked his pulse, still too high, but not, Cal guessed, as bad as it had been. She was now wrapping a blood-pressure cuff around the child's arm.

Would he need fluid replacement?

'His name's Marty,' Jen offered, and Marty's mother, who was sitting beside the little boy and clutching desperately to one hand, turned and nodded.

'I'm sorry, I should have told you that. I don't know what I'm thinking of, except this was such a shock. He had a reaction to peanut butter when he was only eighteen months old and since then we don't have it or peanuts in the house. We've told him and told him they make him really sick, and I honestly thought he understood.'

'The peanuts didn't look like peanuts,' Jen reminded her. 'He might not have known.'

The woman didn't seem appeased, and Cal guessed she was blaming herself for the episode.

'At least this time he might be old enough to remember how sick they made him, so he's less likely to cheat again,' he suggested.

'Blood pressure's within acceptable limits,' the nurse announced, and Cal was relieved. The surge of histamine through the blood at the time of an allergic reaction could cause fluid imbalance which immediately impacted on blood pressure.

But, thanks to Jenny's quick thinking, this seemed to have been averted. He turned to tell his daughter this and saw the new arrival walk through the door.

'I think you'll be needed for speeches,' Blythe said to him, while her brown eyes scanned the small room and took in the situation.

'Allergic reaction? Anaphylactic shock?' she guessed, picking up the discarded ampoule and reading the label on it. 'You go, I'll stay. When did you give him this?'

Cal checked his watch.

'Six minutes ago—you can repeat it any time you like now, but I doubt it's necessary.'

He turned to the nurse.

'I'm sorry, we didn't have time for introductions. I'm—'

'Callum Whitworth,' she finished for him. 'I knew that, and that you were a doctor. I'm glad you were here, though I've coped with this kind of emergency before.' She put out her hand. 'I'm Meg Molloy.'

Cal shook her hand, then introduced Blythe. Marty's mother then joined in the introductions, but Cal sensed impatience in the woman who'd now sidled around to stand beside him.

'They're waiting for you,' Blythe reminded him. 'And

the bride has been known to throw a tantrum when things don't go her way.'

Cal grinned at the caustic comment and excused himself, taking Jen's hand and leading her back to the marquee. He was reasonably certain Meg would be able to handle the child from now on, but having a doctor there as well would soothe the mother.

He returned to his place at the table, smiled reassuringly at the bride, nodded in response to Mark's querying look, then realised, without the bridesmaid by his side to liven up proceedings with her quick wit, he was going to be doomed to a boring session of speeches.

'And I bet Blythe realised that,' he muttered to himself, as the bishop rose to bless the union of the happy couple.

Cal stood obediently, and raised his glass to the two of them then settled back to listen to Mark's rhapsodies. The speech looked like it would be going on for two days, until some ribald comments from the back of the marquee—to the effect of never getting her to the bridal bed if he didn't stop yapping—made the proud groom hurry things along.

Cal knew what came next. Mark proposed a toast to the bridesmaid and it was his place to respond on her behalf, though right now the bridesmaid was conspicuous by her absence.

He was wondering how to explain when the green-clad figure slipped into the seat beside him.

'Some chap who says he's with the RFDS came. He was checking out a stockman who'd burnt his arm last week and came up to the clinic when he'd finished.'

She reached out and took a sip of water and Cal remembered someone telling him his grandfather had arranged for the Royal Flying Doctor Service to have a plane on the ground at Mount Spec while the big crowd was assembled at the station.

It wouldn't be taking anything away from the service as

the plane and staff would still be on call for emergencies in other parts of the Territory, and no doubt his grandfather had made a substantial donation to the RFDS to have the security of a medical officer present. Though with Mark and himself both here, did they need another doctor?

Perhaps it was an indication that his grandfather was still unhappy over his decision to go into medicine...

'What are you frowning about? Surely not your speech?'

Blythe's question was almost drowned out by the applause as Mark finally finished talking.

Cal stood and lifted his glass, raising it to his partner.

'Keep it short,' the person he was representing muttered at him.

He kept it short, but the people who followed him weren't as forbearing, rambling on for what seemed like ages.

'Now surely they're done,' he whispered to Blythe, when some friend of Mark's from his high school days had finally sat down.

'Unless there's someone he went to kindergarten with,' she retorted. 'I'm sorry I didn't have the champagne. I'm sure that last fellow would have sounded funnier if I'd been totally inebriated. I mean, he must have sounded funny to someone. People kept laughing.'

'Other people Mark went to school with, I bet,' Cal told her, then was interrupted by Jenny for a second time.

'Dad, Sam says we're not going to you for Christmas, and you promised this year we could. He says now Mark's married you'll have to shift out of the house, and without Mrs Robertson to look after us and cook dinner and stuff, we can't come.'

Jenny's grey eyes, eerily familiar from his daily view of his own in the mirror, were pleading with him to deny it, but although he hadn't said anything about the holidays, he'd been wondering how to break it to the children that he might not be able to have them.

As he tried to find a noncommittal answer, he was aware of an increased interest on his left-hand side. The bridesmaid was listening very closely and, no doubt, preparing some cutting remark should he be foolish enough to disappoint his daughter.

'Of course you'll still come to me,' he assured Jenny, and had his reward in a radiant smile. She danced triumphantly back to her table, and waggled her fingers to him as she sat down.

'Well, at least you've made someone happy today!' Blythe remarked.

The sting in the tail of the remark added to his gloom.

'She's probably more pleased about proving Sam wrong than coming to me for the holidays,' he said. 'Last time they came to Creamunna they complained non-stop about how boring it was and how there was nothing to do. But at least with Mrs Robertson, Mark's housekeeper, there, they were fed regularly and well. Mark's been assuming I'll stay on in the house, but once he and Lileth return—'

'*If* he and Lileth return,' his partner reminded him. 'Did you get a locum for the time Mark will be away? Maybe he or she will like the place and be willing to stay on.'

Cal turned to her and shook his head.

'A locum? What planet did you drop from?' he demanded. 'Haven't you heard about the difficulties of getting doctors to serve in the bush—about the plight of rural communities who can't get any kind of regular medical services? Why do you think Mark was working on his own for so long? He had to wait until a new chum like me, who actually likes living in the bush, came along.'

A little crease, not large enough to call a frown, had skewed one honey-coloured eyebrow and once again the thought of kissing her sabotaged Cal's brain.

'New chum?' Blythe's question brought him back to reality. 'You're hardly a youngster—what are you—thirty-eight? Forty? Why are you a new chum?'

Cal sighed. He'd carefully got away from this conversation much earlier, but now they'd come full circle.

'I'm only thirty-six,' he began, deciding he needed to get that straight from the start. 'I started late.' He shook his head at the waiter who was offering to fill his glass. 'And before you launch into a series of questions about either my career or my private life, I think you should see what Lileth wants. She's been trying to attract your attention for a few minutes.'

Blythe was happy to escape. Somehow she'd managed to eat a little of her meal and, hopefully, function like a rational human, but the man had set all her nerve endings in a tizz, and it had been a considerable effort to maintain what might pass for polite conversation.

OK, so she'd had lapses, she admitted to herself as she followed Lileth to a tented powder room. But on the whole she felt she'd done quite well.

'Where did you and Callum disappear to?'

The first question was fired at Blythe with such an unmistakable note of censure Blythe had to bite back the urge to make a totally inappropriate reply.

Instead, she meekly explained the situation with the sick child.

But far from offering thanks or praise, Lileth pressed on with her interrogation.

'Where did you get the dress?' was the next question, as the bride subsided onto a chair so Blythe could fix some loose flowers in her hair.

Blythe briefly considered the truth then ruthlessly dismissed it—going for an evasion that wasn't quite a lie.

'Grace provided it,' she said, crossing her fingers and hoping Grace and Lileth hadn't spoken.

'How are you getting on with Cal?'

Boy! Three minutes, three questions, and all of them doozeys!

'It might be easier to take one of the flowers out altogether,' Blythe said, knowing any changes to her appearance on this special day would distract Lileth.

'Which one?'

'Maybe this bud here, then I can use the hair pins from it to secure the loose one.'

So the big question was averted and by the time Blythe accompanied her stepsister back to the table, the change in music indicated it was time for dancing.

'Will the safety pins stand up to some gentle movement around the floor?' Cal asked as, with the formal part of the wedding completed, the bride and groom took centre stage on the small dance-floor. 'I mightn't know the etiquette book by heart, but I remember enough from my own long-ago foray down the aisle to know we're expected to join the happy couple.'

'And you reckon I'm cynical!' Blythe retorted. 'Anyway, you put the pins in place so be it on your own head if they come loose.'

He chuckled and stood up, holding her chair as she rose to her feet. Then she was in his arms and being whirled, albeit gingerly, around the small floor. Years of dance lessons and using dance routines for exercise ensured her feet moved in time to the music and stayed out of reach of his, but they were the only parts of her body behaving with decency and decorum. The rest of her wanted to lean into the man, to feel the solidity of his body against hers, while her mind took flight into the realm of unreality where the mildest of the fantasies owed much to Cinderella's attendance at the Prince's ball.

'The music's stopped.'

The fairy-tale came to an abrupt end, and she stepped hastily away from her partner.

'Good music,' she muttered, hoping he'd think the fairly innocuous tunes produced by the disc jockey who'd replaced the string quartet would explain her distraction.

The silence which greeted this remark made her look directly at him. He wasn't smiling, though his face looked relaxed, but his eyes had a puzzled wariness, easily recognisable as it was much the way she felt herself.

'Dance with your old man?'

Brian's voice made her turn and by the time she looked back to excuse herself, Cal had disappeared.

Brian danced well, and she knew his steps, so she was able to concentrate her mental efforts on why Cal was affecting her the way he was.

He was certainly good-looking but she'd worked with good-looking men at the hospital day in and day out.

He was tall, and well built, but so were at least a proportion of those same men.

He was hardly a sparkling conversationalist—being more argumentative than she was, which was saying something. And he certainly hadn't shown the slightest indication he might be interested in her!

So why had her body wanted to lean on him? Why were her nerves skittering about under her skin like electricity across a pool of water?

'Frustration?'

She realised she'd answered her own question aloud when Brian corrected her.

'No, dear, it's not so much frustration as lack of time to make suitable arrangements.'

Suitable arrangements?

Images of herself clad in a black silk negligee, lounging back against satin pillows, popped obligingly into Blythe's mind.

She stared blankly at her stepfather, hoping she hadn't blurted out more of her thoughts.

'Mumps or not, Mary-Lynne has to be in Sydney on Tuesday,' he said, apparently continuing the conversation Blythe had missed while considering Cal Whitworth and black silk negligees. 'She doesn't have to go into her office, but with her home computer she can finalise all the details of the deal and it can go ahead.'

Mary-Lynne worked in the finance industry, putting together parcels of obscene amounts of money for huge development projects.

'So what's the problem?' Blythe asked, relieved to find she wasn't in the spotlight.

'She doesn't want to fly back in her grandfather's plane with the other wedding guests—being swollen and them all knowing about it. She says she wouldn't feel right.'

'She can fly back to Darwin on the mail plane with me tomorrow, then on a regular airline flight from there. It won't worry me and she's not contagious—well, not highly so—so there shouldn't be a problem with the airline.'

'Except there are no seats available on the mail plane or on any flights out of Darwin until Wednesday even if she could get there,' Brian said, the music ending in time for Blythe to hear the mournful note in his voice. 'That's why we wondered, your mother and I, if you'd be so kind... Lorice is asking Callum now and I said I'd talk to you...'

'I think I'd better sit down,' Blythe told him. 'I can't make head or tail of this conversation. Later, someone can explain it to me, but not until I've had some of that coffee I can smell.'

Still muttering about Callum and Mary-Lynne, Brian escorted her back to her seat then, after a brief, despairing smile, departed.

'Sway back notwithstanding, your mother can dance,' Cal said, dropping into the chair beside her. 'Must be where you get it! But she insisted on more lively steps—she's left me breathless.'

Blythe, who'd been hoping for enlightenment rather than praise for her mother's footwork, studied him. A slight sheen of sweat made the dark hair cling more closely to his head, exaggerating the fine shape of his skull.

'That's it?' she said, when he'd nodded yes to coffee and fixed it to his apparent satisfaction. 'She danced well? Didn't she ask you something? Talk about something?'

The grey eyes blinked, perhaps surprised by her vehemence, then he grinned.

'Oh, about giving you a lift to Creamunna? Well, she did mention it, but I told her you were so crotchety and argumentative you'd make the journey a nightmare instead of a delight, and she understood.'

Blythe was so astounded by the first revelation, she was able to ignore the insults that followed it.

'Give me a lift to Creamunna? I remember Lileth talking about the place. Why in heaven's name would I want a lift to that one-horse town?'

The grin widened into a real smile.

'One-doctor town at present—that's a fair enough comment—but as for horses, we've got dozens of them!'

Blythe felt the anger of frustration—a different frustration—swelling in her chest.

'I do not care how many horses you might or might not have, I have no desire to go to Creamunna!'

She spaced the words out so even a dim-witted doctor would understand them, but was he fazed? No way! He continued to smile—in fact, he gave a little chuckle.

'Can't say I blame you,' he said, his voice positively oozing sympathy. 'Very small town without much going for it. I guess that's why it can't get medical personnel.'

She wanted to shake him, though, given his size, such a move would be physically impossible.

'I don't care about your town or its problems. What I want to know is why my mother would think I'd want to go there?'

'Have some coffee. It might calm you down—or at least give you a breathing space. You look as if you're hyperventilating right now.'

Hyperventilating? Of course she was! She bit back a scream of frustrated rage—damn, there was that word again!

'Apparently, Mary-Lynne needs to get to Sydney, but doesn't want to fly in the plane with other guests.'

'I know that much!' Blythe told him, hoping he'd recognise icy disdain when he heard it in a voice.

'So one solution is that she takes your place on the mail plane and flies via Darwin to Brisbane on your ticket and thence to Sydney, while you come to Creamunna with me—'

'I've heard that bit of the grand plan as well,' Blythe snapped. 'It's the why Creamunna that needs answering.'

Cal smiled triumphantly at her.

'Because there's a bus out of town—you'll be that much closer to home and the bus only takes twelve hours to Brisbane, but of course Mary-Lynne, swollen and ill, couldn't sit on the bus, so her coming with me wouldn't have worked. Your mother explained it all most clearly and, reluctant though I may be to put up with your prickly company, it did make sense.'

Blythe felt her head spinning.

'It's ''please, Blythe'' all over again!' she muttered. It occurred to her she could have done a direct swap with Mary-Lynne, taking her seat in the private plane, but that would land her in Sydney late at night with no clothes, and she'd have to fork out for a hotel room as well as a flight back to Brisbane.

Unfortunately, she could see her mother's impeccable logic in the new arrangement, but that didn't make her feel any better.

Neither did the prospect of travelling from one remote bit of the outback to another remote bit of it, in the company of Callum Whitworth, fill her with unalloyed joy. In fact, what she felt was more like apprehension, but when he asked her to dance again, she found herself saying yes.

CHAPTER THREE

ONCE back in Cal's arms, Blythe found the desire to lean had developed into an urge to snuggle—definitely not good. Maybe it was time to put her new approach to men into action—to try out her love 'em and leave 'em plan. It was, in fact, a perfect situation, being attracted to a man she'd never see after tonight—or tomorrow at the very latest.

But was it wise to launch this new-Blythe procedure with someone who was almost family?

A step-cousin?

Probably not.

To distract her mind from these close-to-out-of-control thoughts and her body from its unseemly behaviour, she tracked back through the conversation, and thought about the bus trip instead. She'd never heard of Creamunna until Lileth had headed off in that direction, but she was reasonably sure it was in Queensland.

And Cal had said it was closer to Brisbane than where they were now.

But twelve hours by bus?

The shudder of horror which shook her must have been strong enough for Cal to feel it, for he tucked her closer, and not snuggling became more difficult. OK, so say a bus averages eighty kilometres an hour, multiply that by twelve—

'Are you praying? Is my dancing that bad?'

Startled by the questions, Blythe glanced up in time to catch the amusement in his grey eyes. It softened them, and implied an intimacy she found physically disturbing.

'Your lips were moving,' he added, perhaps thinking her silence meant she hadn't understood his questions.

She eased a little away from him, rallying all her common sense to her defence.

'I was working out how far Creamunna must be from Brisbane—you know, twelve hours at—'

'About a thousand kilometres,' he said, and as the music shifted to a slow, dreamy beat, he drew her close again, so the question of how long they had to drive to get to Creamunna, from here in the vastness of the Northern Territory, remained unasked.

Fighting the insidious effects of physical attraction to the man took all her wits, so that part of the equation remained a mystery. But if they left after the wedding, and one or other of them was driving at all times, then there'd be no opportunity for the new-Blythe stuff to happen.

Which was probably just as well.

In an effort to regain some control over her wayward senses, she then danced with any man who asked her, ignoring dire warnings about pins popping from her companion whenever she returned to the table.

When the bride and groom departed, and guests were free to stay and mingle, Cal loomed up behind Blythe as she stood talking to Brian's nephew, Paul Reynolds, who was one of a small group of the Bell family friends who'd trekked into the country for the big event.

'I'll be leaving in half an hour if you want that lift,' Cal growled. 'I'll check on young Marty then call by the shearers' quarters, and if you're there you can come. If you're not I go without you.'

He strode away, obviously angry about something, before she could reply.

'Charming company he's going to be!' she said to Paul. 'But if he's bent on leaving soon I'd better find Mum and Brian to say goodbye.'

Undoing the pins took most of the allotted time, then there was the problem of what to do with the curtain. In the end, Blythe folded it and tucked it into the shoulder-bag she'd carried with her on her journey north and west. She'd see if she could replace it in Brisbane and send a new one back to Grace with an explanation and apology.

Clad in her jeans and the T-shirt, and wishing this *was* one of her more adequate moments, she stood outside the small room that had been hers for the past twenty-four hours.

When the golf buggy approached, she ignored it, looking beyond it for a real car, but it pulled up directly in front of her and, though Cal had changed from his dinner suit into jeans and a checked shirt, there was no mistaking the driver or his order to get in.

Oh, no! This time her mother had definitely gone too far. She bent so she could see her chauffeur.

'There is no way I am driving across half of Australia in this thing!' she told him.

He gave her the incredulous kind of look usually reserved for wondrous animals at the zoo.

'Get in, you stupid woman,' he roared. 'Of course you're not driving across the bloody country in this thing. For a start it's electric and the battery would die before we reached the front gate.'

Blythe got in, but she had no intention of swallowing his insults.

'Then how do they get around golf courses, if they've got so little power in their batteries?'

Her triumphant glare had no effect on him whatsoever. He simply started the vehicle and they rolled away.

'It's about four times as far to our front gate as it is around a golf course,' he said, waving an acknowledgement to a man who'd opened a gate for them.

Thus squelched, Blythe folded her hands in her lap and

her lips tightly over her teeth so she didn't say anything else stupid, and took a look around. It had been dusk last night when the mail plane had landed, so she'd managed to get only a vague idea of the layout of the place. Now they were passing cattle yards, and more sheds than she could believe would be necessary. Trucks, motor bikes, utilities and tractors, all manner of machinery seemed to be needed for a business of this size.

They stopped at another gate, this one closed, and she knew enough country lore to hop out and open it, then wait until Cal drove through, and close it again.

She contemplated asking where they were going, but Cal's set lips and grim expression suggested she'd be better keeping quiet. Until she saw where they were heading—the line-up of small planes on the strip were testament to how many people in the outback used air transport to get around.

'We're flying? You fly?'

The words stuttered from her lips.

'My plane's a four-seater—not that much smaller than the mail plane,' he said, perhaps assuming the idea of flying in a small plane had frightened her.

'But your parents—the girls' mother—how...?'

'How could I take to the air when my parents had died in a crash?'

He put it so bluntly, all she could do was nod acknowledgement of her thoughts.

'People whose family members are killed in car accidents still drive, you know. And out here, if you want to get somewhere in less than twenty-four hours, it's the only way to go.'

Blythe swallowed her own apprehension about travelling in small planes. If this man, given his history, could do it, then so could she.

'Scared?'

The question told Blythe she hadn't quite hidden her fear, but she wasn't going to admit it.

'Me? Scared? You've got to be joking.'

She was about to launch into an elaborate and totally fictitious tale of her experience in small plane trips when Cal stopped the buggy and climbed out beside a plane not much bigger than the earthbound vehicle.

Blythe closed her eyes and opened them again, but it hadn't grown any larger. She comforted herself with the thought that terror would probably provide an effective dampener for the sexual attraction she'd been feeling towards the man and moved, on legs stiff with apprehension, towards the little plane.

Which Cal proceeded to push away from her, so she had to follow it like someone hurrying after a bus.

'Move it. We've only a few hours of light, and though I'm qualified to land in darkness there are no lights on our strip so I want to get home earlier rather than later.'

She hurried to close the gap between them.

'Put your foot here,' he said when he'd positioned the craft where he wanted it. He swung open a hatch-like door and indicated an indentation in the outer skin of the plane which was apparently intended as a step. 'I'll give you a boost if you can't pull yourself up.'

Determined not to need the 'boost', she put her foot where he'd indicated and grabbed a hand grip to pull herself into the seat. But she had the wrong foot on the step, and before she could change it, large firm hands clasped her bottom and lifted her, all but flinging her into the seat.

'Well, really!' she muttered as he slammed the door then walked around the plane to get in beside her.

But he took no notice of her, simply working his way through what must have been some kind of pre-take-off ritual, barking an order to her about fastening her seat belt, before the little machine moved off up the runway and rose effortlessly into the air.

Beneath them, the ground dropped away, the house and bungalows grew smaller, and around them the day seemed brighter, though in the west the approaching sunset was starting to paint the sky with vivid colour. But once they'd left the cluster of buildings the vast emptiness of the land beneath them forced her into speech.

'How do you know where you're going?' she asked, pitching her voice to get above the engine noise.

Cal swung a smile her way.

'Sky map,' he told her, then pointed to an instrument panel. 'I set the course we'll fly on these, although even without instruments I've flown this route often enough to know every bump and twist in the landscape.'

There was joy in his voice, clear and unmistakable, and Blythe relaxed, looking around her as she tried to capture a little of what it was Cal felt.

'It seems so impossible—being up here in a tiny capsule of metal and moving through the air at speed.'

'Magic, isn't it?'

Again the joy, but this time accompanied by a smile, which reminded her of the attraction she'd hoped fear would keep at bay. But try as she may to recover just a little apprehension, both mind and body refused to play along. In fact, they were revelling in the experience. Well, her mind revelled in the flight, while her body—best she didn't think about what it was feeling!

'We're crossing the border about now, back into Queensland. The flight takes less than two hours, so we'll be home just after sunset.'

'Home? After one year, is it home to you?'

He glanced her way as if surprised by the question, then checked his instruments again and peered out through his window towards the ground over which they flew.

'Yes, I think it is,' he said, when she'd begun to think he wasn't going to answer at all. 'When I started hospital work during my student years, I really loved anaesthetics. I even considered specialising—you know, big wheel in a big hospital. But not for long.'

He grinned at her.

'I guess you know the old saying about being able to take the boy out of the country but not being able to take the country out of the boy? I found myself pining for wide open spaces and, much as I loved the work in big hospitals, I hated the city.'

'You could have been a specialist in a big regional town,' she pointed out, and received another grin. The man was obviously happy, up here in the sky. Or perhaps it was the emptiness over which they flew that was meeting his need for 'country'.

'Compromise?' He shook his head. 'A big regional town—one large enough to have specialists—is just a smaller city. Besides, they are all either along the coast or in the rich farming belt immediately beyond it. They're in placid green country. I wanted real rural medicine—a place where I felt I was needed, and able to achieve something. And I also wanted this!'

He waved his hand towards the nothingness beneath them. 'Red desert country. Spinifex country. Heat and dust and praying for rain, then the lush beauty when it comes, the great renewal after floods.'

'Sounds to me like there's a wide streak of masochism in your genetic make-up!' Blythe told him. 'Or perhaps insanity!'

But her rudeness failed to dim his obvious happiness, so vital she could feel it in the small space they shared.

Though she didn't feel it diminish in any way and was only alerted to trouble when a loud, though not offensive swear word rent the air.

'Look for somewhere flat and treeless. This area has salt pans—they're a whitish colour, the bottom of lakes formed in floods.'

Medical training had ensured Blythe could obey orders without question, so she peered out and down, looking ahead and out to her side of the plane.

A large whitish area stretched away to her left. No dark blobs indicating trees seemed to mar its surface.

'Over there.' She touched his arm and pointed, then felt a little spurt of pleasure as he turned the plane in that direction.

The stubby trees on the desert plain around the whitish patch grew bigger as they lost altitude and the sudden silence told her that whatever had happened to cause this emergency landing had killed the engine.

'Lean forward and fold your arms around your knees, holding yourself in as compact a ball as you can,' Cal ordered.

'What about you?' she demanded, although she was already obeying him. 'How do you protect yourself?'

She twisted her head to see his face, so saw the smile he flashed her.

'Prayer?'

It was the last thing she remembered before they slammed onto the ground, then jolted unnervingly across a surface rougher than it had looked from above.

'As soon as we stop, unbuckle your harness and get out. Fast!'

Cal's voice was tight and strained, but before she could check how he looked, the little plane somersaulted, flipping onto its nose then flopping over onto its back so they were both hanging by their seat belts like bats settling in for their daytime sleep.

An ominous quiet from her companion made her glance his way, but she wasted no time with questions.

Get your harness off! The order had been clear. Disorientated though she was, Blythe found the clasp and released it, then dropped head first to the ceiling of the plane. She fumbled for the doorhandle. If Cal was OK he'd be doing the same, and if he wasn't, the sooner she was out and able to help him, the better.

The door wouldn't open, so she twisted until she could brace herself against the seat and slammed her feet into it. The pain in her ankles made her wince, but the effort was effective. The door opened.

Now she could turn to Cal, who certainly wasn't doing anything about getting out. Though he did have a pulse, which was reassuring given he was the only person present who knew anything about planes, the bush and how to get help.

'Hang tight,' she told him. 'If I can get your door open, it might be easier to manoeuvre you out when I release you from your harness. Sort of drop you straight onto the ground—though preferably not on your head.'

She slid out herself, clutching her shoulder-bag, which had been on her knee during the flight. Leaking fuel, fire danger—get everyone away from the source of danger. Training in emergency situations brought lists of procedures to mind as Blythe sniffed the air, praying whatever might happen next wouldn't happen until she had Cal out of the plane.

His door opened easily, making her wonder if planes might be constructed with accidents in mind.

'Nonsense!' she told herself, speaking aloud to reassure herself. 'If doors opened too easily you'd fall out in mid-air. Anyway, they're probably called hatches.'

She studied his position, but she didn't have the technical skills to work out where and how he'd fall when she released him, so in the end she unsnapped the harness catch and hoped for the best. Though she did put her bag with the folded curtain in it as extra padding where she thought his head was most likely to land.

His body crumpled limply down onto the plane's ceiling—did planes have ceilings?—but in such a manner his legs were freed, so they tipped sideways out of the plane and she was able to use them to drag his body on to the ground.

'Not doing much for your concussion, bumping your head around like this,' she told him apologetically, but as he was still out to it he failed to respond, making Blythe suddenly feel very, very alone.

He'd had a bag with him—perhaps with some medical equipment in it?

She clambered in but the bag was entangled in the mesh luggage restraint and she was still too concerned about fire to untangle it. There was a rough bushman's coat in there as well, and when she tugged at it, it came free. Tough oilskin. If she could roll his body onto it, she could shift him further from the plane, though perhaps if it was going to blow up it would have done so by now.

The thought of an imminent explosion added panic to her haste, and she rolled the upper half of Cal's body onto the jacket then, grasping it by the collar, managed to drag him, slow inch by slow inch, a little further from the plane.

'Now, if I swing your legs around...'

A low groan disturbed her planning, and she dropped to her knees, embarrassed to think she'd ignored his physical state for so long.

'Cal! Can you hear me? Do you know your name?'

Stupid damn question when she'd just told him his name!

'Cal!' she called louder, and heard her own despair echo in the sound.

He groaned again but didn't answer.

With fingers trembling from the realisation of her isolation, she felt his head, found the lump that explained his unconscious state but felt no movement of bone beneath her fingers.

'Not that anything but an X-ray would show up a fracture,' she muttered to herself.

'Not even then sometimes,' a voice reminded her, and she looked down to see his eyes open, the steely hued gaze fixed enquiringly on her face.

'I know you, don't I?' he added. 'You're the wrong bridesmaid.'

'And who are you?' Blythe asked him, while telling herself the uproar in the region of her heart was caused by relief that he was conscious again, not by the way his eyes had suddenly smiled into hers.

'Checking me out, Doctor?' The eyes were still smiling as he answered her question with a question. 'I'm Callum Whitworth, pilot of plane that's just landed you, safely I hope, in the middle of nowhere.' The smile became concern. 'You *are* all right?'

Blythe nodded, which was a safer option than speaking, given how unstable the smiling eyes had made her feel.

'Well, I'd better get up from this comfortable bed and see what's what. I don't suppose you got the Epirb going?'

Not knowing what an Epirb was, let alone how to get one going, she stuck to muteness, simply shaking her head.

But when Cal tried to sit up, then swore and slumped awkwardly back to the ground, she reacted swiftly.

'What is it, where are you hurting? If it's your back, don't try to move. Damn! I didn't even check your spine before I got you out!'

He summoned up a smile, though it didn't improve the pinched whiteness of his features.

'Better to end up a live paraplegic than be burned to death had the plane gone up. You did the right thing. But it's not my back, it's my arm—or maybe my shoulder.

When we hit, the stick was all but wrenched from my grasp. I guess I held on a bit too tight.'

Blythe must have looked anxious for he added gently, 'I'm OK now. Be a good girl and help me into a sitting position. Once there, I'll soon be on my feet.'

'Which shoulder?' Blythe asked, not touching him until she knew more.

'Right!' His voice was tight with pain, but he insisted on moving, so Blythe squatted on his left side, slid her hand under his neck and very cautiously eased him up into a sitting position.

His face lost its last vestiges of colour during this operation and, fearing he'd faint again, she decided to take charge.

'Tell me where this Epirb thing is and what it looks like. You'll be more use to this enterprise giving orders than passing out every two minutes.'

Again he summoned up a smile.

'And to think I took you for a woman who wouldn't take kindly to orders!'

She used a glare which had cowed erring junior staff but had no effect at all on Cal, who continued to grin at her as if she was some kind of humorous apparition.

'The Epirb!' she reminded him.

'It's a flat red box in the mesh map holder between the seats. I should have set it going before we came down— damn stupid of me not to have considered it, but the clay plan looked deceptively flat and I thought we'd land without incident.'

He winced as if his anger at himself had hurt his injury, but Blythe was already clambering back into the plane, orienting herself to its position then finding the mesh holder he'd mentioned.

The flat red contraption was where he'd said it would be, with clear instructions how to activate it.

She brought it out with her, followed the instructions, then hesitated.

'You don't have to stand there holding it. Set it down somewhere out of the way. It transmits a signal to tell people where we are. Once the signal is picked up, a search plane will be sent out, but because it's getting dark no one will reach us in time to get us out tonight, so we need to get a fire going. That way anyone flying over will know we're OK.'

No one will get us out tonight...

Anyone flying over will know we're OK...

'Don't you have a radio? Don't all planes have radios? Couldn't we just call someone up and tell them where we are? If they know exactly, they could come and get us now.'

She looked expectantly at her companion, but if she'd expected praise for this suggestion she was disappointed. He was looking more furious than congratulatory!

'Yes, I have a radio—yes, all planes have them, but even if mine was working, no one would get to us tonight. The closest homestead could be a hundred k's away, and there's nowhere here for a plane to land, so it will be a helicopter that comes eventually.'

Blythe knew she should be pleased about the helicopter, but the rest of the explanation defied belief.

'Your radio isn't working? Isn't it illegal or something to fly without one?'

'Not exactly illegal and I didn't discover it wasn't working until I was due to leave Creamunna yesterday afternoon. Tried to get it going, and in the end I had to fax through my flight plan and phone later to say I'd arrived. It's why I was late arriving at Mount Spec and missed the dinner.'

'Oh!'

There really wasn't much else to say, though she did think of something else and grinned at him.

'Well, at least no one can blame the broken radio on me. I wasn't even there when it happened.'

He smiled back, and Blythe had to remind herself of all the reasons it would not be a good idea to get involved, even briefly, with this man.

'You stay here, I'll scout around for wood.'

The practical statement helped anchor her back to reality. Cal was struggling to his feet as he spoke but the colour drained from his face before he was fully upright and she reached him just in time to prevent a further collapse.

'Sit down, you stupid man. Let me have a look at your shoulder.'

He sat, but when she leaned across him to feel his shoulder, he turned away.

'Leave it be,' he said, and she guessed from the menacing way he spoke it was far more painful than he'd let on. 'There's not a darned thing you can do out here.'

'Of course there is,' she argued automatically. 'If it's dislocated I should be able to get it back in place. If you've damaged ligaments, I can fashion a sling.'

'So I'll have my shoulder nicely tied up but we'll freeze to death without a fire. Concentrate on survival first—anything else can wait.'

Though she hated to admit it, his words made sense.

'OK, *I'll* look for wood.'

She hoped she sounded braver than she felt, but staying on her own near the plane hadn't been that great an option, and at least gathering wood would give her something to take her mind off the 'won't be rescued tonight' scenario.

Darkness was falling fast and she hurried off, picking up sticks, no matter how small, keeping the plane always in sight.

She brought an armload back then decided there was an easier way. Grabbing the curtain from her handbag, she took it with her, stacking her finds on the material then wrapping the lot and carrying back a bigger bundle.

'Grace's curtain still being put to good use, I see?' Cal remarked, when she returned to empty the bundle beside him.

He'd shifted further from the plane and already had a small fire going.

'How did you do that? Rub two sticks together?'

He grinned at her, and held up a cigarette lighter.

'Old bushman's habit—never travel without matches or a lighter that works. I had both in my coat pockets, but had trouble using the matches one-handed.'

Blythe heard the words, but didn't really take them in— too busy working out why his sudden smile had made her legs go wonky. Crashing in a plane could make your legs go wonky, but a man's smile...

She was still working through this when she saw the scored salt-crusted earth between where he'd been and where he was and realised he'd dragged himself about twenty metres.

'What else is wrong?' she asked. Guilt over her negligence in not examining him properly made her voice tight and anxious.

'Ankle!' he said briefly. 'But one-handed I can't feel any broken bones, so I'd say it's just a sprain. Serves me right for flying in these fancy ''going-dancing'' shoes instead of my trusty boots.'

'I'd better have a look,' Blythe said, though, considering the effect his grin had had on her knees, the very last thing she wanted to do was examine this man's body.

'Don't trust my diagnosis?' he teased, but when she knelt beside him he put out a hand to keep her away.

'I know what's wrong and what isn't,' he said, so gently he might almost be apologising for something.

Cal hoped she'd take his word for it. It must be the concussion, or perhaps the brush with death—the isolation? Something had made his body respond to this woman in such an inappropriate manner that to have her touch him would not only be mortifying to him but probably acutely embarrassing to her.

'I know it's getting dark but with the fire to guide you, do you think you might find more wood? As well as providing a reassuring beacon, we'll need it for warmth tonight. Don't go out of sight of it, even momentarily. The plains can be very disorienting.'

Blythe studied him for a moment, as if trying to read something behind his brusque request. No doubt she'd see how much he hated being reliant on her—on anyone— because he'd never been much good at hiding his frustration, whether with himself or others!

Then a little smile touched her lips.

'You, too,' she said. 'No more hauling yourself across the ground. I want you right here by this fire when I get back.'

She stood up, but slowly, and Cal knew she must be feeling pain. Though not as badly damaged as his, her body would have been jolted as they'd landed then flipped over. He had to hand it to her. She mightn't have been first choice of bridesmaid, but she had guts. He was reasonably certain Lileth's blood sister would have been having hysterics rather than heading off into the darkness to gather wood.

'Water! You surely carry water in the plane!'

She returned from an unexpected direction so he had to turn to face her.

'You look like a Valkyrie out of Norse legends—with your firewood clasped to your chest like a shield.'

'Didn't the Valkyrie choose the dead heroes from battlegrounds to take them to Valhalla?' she said, loosening the curtain so the wood fell to the ground. 'You're not dead yet,' she reminded him.

'Nor much of a hero,' he muttered, 'letting you do all the work.'

She waved away his protest, moving back towards the plane.

'Water!' she said, reminding him of her earlier comment. 'Will I find water somewhere in the plane?'

Cal felt a quiver of alarm. Knowledge and experience told him that if the plane was going to go up in flames, it would have done so by now, but he was reluctant to let her go close to it again.

Though he suspected not even an able-bodied man would be able to stop Blythe Jones once she set her mind to something.

'Plastic container strapped down behind the rear seats, and for heaven's sake be careful in there. If you smell fuel don't go near it. We'll survive a night without water.'

She continued on her way, her shape becoming wraith-like in the gloom as she neared the darker shadow of the plane. He pictured it, seats up above her head, the straps holding down the luggage net almost impossible to reach. If she released the wrong one, would the water drum come crashing down on her head?

Anxiety tightened his gut and made his shoulder ache even more, and he cursed his feebleness and immobility. Time dragged—she should have been back by now.

He'd just decided to ignore her orders and haul himself back over to the plane when the crunch of shoes on the salt crust told him she was returning.

His relief was so overwhelming it veered irrationally towards anger and it was only with great fortitude he refrained from snapping at her.

'I fished around in the other paraphernalia you keep back there, thinking you might have some iron rations, but no such luck. Though I brought your bag back in case you fancy a shave or a change of clothes.'

'As if!' he muttered, then realised she was teasing when the firelight revealed a wide smile on her face.

'You can use it as a pillow,' she said. 'I've checked my bag too but, apart from some rather mouldy-looking par-acetemol tablets in a torn foil packet, I can't do much in the way of pain relief. Though if I scrabble around in the bottom of it, I'm almost sure I have a few butterscotch lollies left over from the flight up.'

Blythe dropped in a smooth—and strangely elegant, given the circumstances—movement to sit cross-legged by the fire, then leaned towards it, using the light to peer into the depths of her shoulder-bag.

'Ha! I thought so. Butterscotch. Here's one for you and one for me. We can have these now for dinner and I'll divide up any more we find—breakfast, lunch. Isn't that the way to do it when people go into survival mode?'

Cal was still wondering what to say—apart from thanking her for the sweet she'd pressed into his hand—when she spoke again.

'And a cup—well, it's not exactly a cup but it will do as one. Short of getting you to open your mouth while I poured water into it, I couldn't work out how you'd manage to drink from the drum with only one workable arm.'

She waved what looked like a small plastic beaker at him.

'Vitamin container,' she explained. 'I found a nearly empty bottle of vitamins in the bag as well. We can eat them when the butterscotch run out.'

Crossing back to where she'd left the water, she knelt and carefully filled the small receptacle, then passed it to him.

He felt the tremor in her fingers and realised her spate of cheery conversation could be close to hysteria, but she was coping so bravely he didn't want to say anything that might crack her fragile façade.

'Well, here's to us!' he said, lifting the little cup to salute her. 'And to the resourcefulness of women everywhere who can produce such succour from the bottom of their handbags!'

She smiled and blinked, but rallied quickly, holding out her hand for the cup and refilling it, ordering him to drink more.

'Do you want a couple of paracetemol?' she asked. 'If you're in less pain you might manage some sleep.'

'Later,' he told her, knowing the pain would worsen as shock wore off.

He looked around their makeshift camp, feeling the chill night air already dropping on them. His head ached, his shoulder caused exquisite pain every time he breathed— though that could be explained by a damaged rib—and his ankle throbbed, so trying to work out the logistics for a night in the bush wasn't easy.

'I know you've no spare clothes, but take whatever you can find in my bag and put it on, over what you're wearing. I'll get this coat off and you can have that as well.'

'Nonsense!' the woman he was trying to help said bluntly. 'You stay on the coat—it will give your body some protection from the cold seeping up from the ground. We'll pile the clothes on top of us, and the trusty curtain, of course, and snuggle up.'

'Snuggle up?'

The words were out before he could stop them, and even in the dim light he caught the scathing glance she sent him.

'It's not an assault on your manhood, but a survival

technique. Body heat will work more effectively together than alone. You must know that.'

Of course he knew it but he felt a strong reluctance to snuggle up to Blythe. True, his body was behaving itself—for the moment—but there was no guarantee it would remain quiescent.

Though you'd think the pain he was suffering would be enough to dampen unwanted and unacceptable ardour!

'Of course, I could dig a hole and put you in it, then cover you with ashes. That seems to ring a bell, but perhaps it's to do with roasting pigs, rather than survival.'

Cal shook his head and found himself chuckling at the image she'd evoked.

'I think I'd prefer the snuggling—just in case!' he told her.

CHAPTER FOUR

THOUGH she'd tried to sound quite matter-of-fact about it, Blythe was reluctant to start the snuggling too early, so she settled herself cross-legged by the fire, content to sit a while, looking into the hot red heart of it and watch the flickering patterns of the flames.

It was probably because she'd—though only momentarily—considered Cal for her new love 'em and leave 'em approach to relationships that the idea of snuggling up to him gave her palpitations.

What if, when half-asleep, she snuggled too close?

Gave in to that—again momentary—desire to press against his body.

Get your mind off sex!

Think of something else!

Anything!

She thought about the accident, but that was worse. Try as she may to remind herself that being disaster-prone was a family joke, not an actual, provable, scientific fact, the thought kept insinuating itself into her mind.

And once there, it was so all-encompassing, she'd have been better sticking to her original line of contemplation. Though there was no way—absolutely no way—the accident could have had anything to do with her.

Unless her weight had made a difference—she'd had to give her weight before getting on the mail plane...

Cal sat not far away, occasionally feeding another piece of wood onto the fire but not offering either conversation or argument. So, in the end, she had to ask—if only to relieve the agony of self-doubt her own thoughts were causing.

'What happened? Up there?'

He turned towards her, so she could see his features half-shadowed in the firelight—see his lips teasing into the tiniest of smiles.

'I was carrying a harbinger of doom, of course,' he said, then a real smile flashed across his face. 'I bet that's what you were thinking. It's ridiculous, of course, to allow yourself such fantasies. Things happen, you know, and after they happen it's easy to connect them to something else and see signs and portents.'

Blythe felt a flush of pleasure at this reassurance—well, not so much from the reassurance but because he'd bothered to try to make her feel less responsible. But flushes of pleasure didn't answer the question.

'What things happened in this particular case?' she persisted.

The smile had long gone, but now his expression grew more serious and a puzzled frown marred his ruggedly handsome features.

'I really don't know, but I'd say with the number of planes flying into the station for the wedding, and most of them needing to be refuelled at Mount Spec, the boys have dragged out some old drums of fuel and I've picked up some dirt that's blocked the plane's fuel lines, or some water that's leaked into an old drum or collected through condensation.'

'So no fuel getting through to the engine?'

'Exactly.'

Which finished that short and not particularly promising conversation.

Blythe did a mental scout around other topics, but all the things she really wanted to ask might be considered too personal. She went for professional instead.

'Now we've taken care of survival, shall I look at your shoulder and ankle? Perhaps binding your ankle will relieve some of the pain.'

'It doesn't hurt when I'm just sitting here,' Cal told her.

'But your shoulder must. I can tell from the way you're holding your arm. Have you investigated it? Is it the scapula or the clavicle?'

Cal had investigated it and had heard the crepitation where the broken ends of bone had moved against each other when he'd gingerly fingered his clavicle. A figure-of-eight bandage around his back and shoulders would undoubtedly relieve some of the pain, but for reasons he couldn't explain, even to himself, he didn't want Blythe doing it.

Touching him...

'You're behaving like a child!' she scolded, getting up from her position by the fire and moving determinedly towards him. 'Scared to let me touch you because you know it's going to hurt.'

It isn't the pain that bothers me, Cal thought but didn't say.

She knelt beside him, reminding him in a physical way of all the reasons he didn't want her touching him.

'Now, don't tell me you haven't investigated it. Is there a broken bone?' Her eyes were shadowed but the firelight illuminated her pale skin with a golden glow.

A year in Creamunna, during which time all you've had was one two-week break, and that was with the kids, he reminded himself. It's prolonged celibacy attracting you to this woman.

'The clavicle,' he growled, and read the disbelief in her face.

'Wrenching broke it? If it twisted it will be a comminuted break likely to have loose bits of bone floating free.'

She had her hands on his shirt and he could smell butterscotch on her breath as she leaned cautiously over his injured shoulder, careful not to touch him with anything but the very lightest of light hands.

Which moved down his arm to his hand, where she pinched him lightly on the wrist.

'Ouch!'

'Had to check nerve involvement,' she murmured, cradling his fingers in her hand and lifting it towards the fire.

'The blood's flowing both ways—no swelling, no coldness, no discoloration,' he told her, trying to retrieve the hand she'd captured but unable to pull it away from her because of the pain in his shoulder.

'You're the patient, I'm the doctor,' she reminded him. 'But you're right—it seems OK. Now, about that bandage. I can tear the curtain into strips and use that to do a figure of eight around your shoulder, and there should be a bit left over to fashion a sling of sorts. You think it's likely to get cold tonight so I'll put it over your shirt.'

Cal opened his mouth to argue but she'd moved away, producing the curtain again from the seemingly bottomless handbag and proceeding to tear it into strips, using sharp white teeth to get each division started.

'I'll do a couple extra for your ankle,' she said, handing him a bunch of strips and a larger piece, no doubt intended for a sling.

'My ankle's fine as it is,' Cal grumbled.

'And one more for your mouth—a gag to stop you arguing!'

He hoped she was joking, though the set expression on her face suggested otherwise. Why a set expression? If she was indeed a doctor, then tying up a broken shoulder shouldn't make her frown.

'We'll be all right, you know,' he said, thinking she might be more worried about their situation than she was letting on. Worry would explain the frown. 'There'll be a

search and rescue helicopter landing here at first light—
you wait and see.'

'I'll have to, won't I?' she joked, but although she
smiled he imagined he could hear strain in her voice.

Blythe knelt beside him again, and reached into his lap
to take a strip of curtain.

'Can you hold it in place while I do the first loop?' she
asked, starting with the end on his uninjured shoulder.

As he reached up to take it, his fingers brushed hers and
he felt a tremor he suspected was as much hers as his. He
longed to comfort her, to say something to make things
better, but as he didn't know words enough to help, he
took the quivering fingers in his hand and lifted them to
his lips, pressing a kiss into the soft palm of her hand.

'You've been wonderful,' he said, releasing her hand as
she tried to tug it free. 'Here you are, calmly bandaging
me up, when most women would be having hysterics, or
at the very least weeping copiously.'

'You don't have a very high opinion of women, do
you?' she remarked, reaching around his body with the
length of material. 'There, I'll knot it low down so the
knot doesn't press into the injured part.'

He could feel the softness of her breasts against his
back, and smell the fragrance of her hair as it brushed
against his face. It made him think things he shouldn't
think—especially about a colleague who was treating him.

But her arms wrapped around him like a lover's, and
for the first time in many, many years he felt a sense of
loneliness.

'It must be Mark marrying that brought it on,' he mumbled to himself, then realised he was voicing thoughts he
shouldn't be having. Perhaps a reaction to shock!

'Brought what on?' Blythe asked, knotting another strip
of cloth to the bandage and winding it expertly across his
back. 'Your poor opinion of women?'

'Of course not. It was just a remark, and nothing to do with women.'

Not much!

Arms reached around again, but this time pain stopped him thinking unacceptable thoughts.

'Hurts, doesn't it?' Blythe said, no doubt responding to his wince. 'But I had to put some pressure on to pull your shoulders back. That should counteract the downwards displacement of bone.'

'And probably cut off my venous flow!' Pain added venom to his voice.

'I've still got the gag if you get cheeky,' she reminded him, but the hands that tucked the end of the bandage in and fitted the sling were gentle, and when she stood up, leaving the coolness of the evening pressing on his back, the sense of loneliness he'd felt earlier returned.

'Now your ankle,' she announced, but he put out his good hand to stop her.

'No, truly, it's all right.'

'Then why won't you let me touch it? For a start I should take off your shoe. If the ankle's swelling, the shoe could cause constriction to the blood vessels.'

She was right, of course, which made him feel worse, not better. He tried to remember if Grace had ever fussed over him.

Perhaps when they were first married? He'd certainly been injured often enough. Falls from the motorbike when a mob of cattle had turned too quickly, or he'd hit an unseen rut in the grass and been thrown through the air. The other men laughing—their way of showing sympathy—roughly checking he'd had no broken bones before getting on with the job.

Blythe lifted his ankle, gently easing off his shoe, and pain stopped further thought.

'Could be a sprain or perhaps a Pott's fracture,' she told

him, as her fingers pressed into the skin just above his ankle.

'That covers a lot of ground,' he told her, trying to draw his foot away from her as her explorations were causing more pain than he wanted to handle right now.

'Yes,' she agreed, resting his ankle back on the ground. 'But it's handy to have something to say to a patient. I mean, a Potts fracture sounds simple compared to "an isolated fracture of the lateral malleolus", now, doesn't it? Say that to a patient and he or she would immediately freak out because it sounds so much more serious than good old Potts.'

Cal found himself chuckling as she reached for another strip of material from his lap, though what lay ahead should have deadened any amusement.

'Let's leave it until it's been X-rayed,' he suggested, knowing the process of binding the ankle would hurt like hell, even if it did feel better later.

'And risk displacement of the bones if there is a fracture? If it's a simple break with no displacement, all you'll need is a walking cast for three to six weeks, but once the bones move you're going to need a general anaesthetic and manipulation—'

Blythe stopped so abruptly he forgot he'd been about to tell her to teach her grandmother to suck eggs, and instead demanded, 'What? What's wrong?'

'Where will the helicopter take us? I was thinking we'd finish up at Creamunna, but you need a doctor—and as you're the only doctor in town for the moment, there's no point in taking you there. And what will happen to your patients while you're laid up? Will the RFDS cover for you?'

Cal closed his eyes. The knock on his head must have affected him more badly than he'd realised. He hadn't even considered the immediate consequences of this accident.

Well, beyond getting rescued!

'Mark's experience when he took a break was that the Flying Doctors will cover emergencies. They do that anyway, flying out people who need urgent specialist care. Day-to-day stuff the sisters at the hospital handle, or people travel to the Derryville, the nearest large town. Damn, but this is a mess!'

'And you've got your kids arriving.' Blythe's reminder fired an anger born of frustration.

'Not until Christmas—that's months away—but thank you, little ray of sunshine, for that timely reminder,' he growled. 'Anything else you'd like to add to my load of troubles?'

'*Your* troubles?' she said, the inflection in her voice giving new meaning to the word 'scathing'. 'What about mine? Stuck out here in the wilderness with a misogynistic medico—an injured misogynistic medico at that—and no hope of rescue till morning, which means I'll probably miss the bus to Brisbane, and with my luck there won't be another one for days, and no matter what you say, my entire family will blame me for this disaster. Then on top of that, all I had to eat at lunch was the entrée, then a lettuce leaf and a slice of chicken, because after the experience of the bridesmaid's dress I was dreading the pins might give way, so I'm starving.'

'And to think you gave me one of your butterscotches,' Cal said, trying hard not to laugh at Blythe's litany of woes.

'Yes,' she said, quite seriously he thought, though it was hard to tell in the firelight. 'That was stupid of me, wasn't it? Well, as thanks for my largesse, let me bind this ankle. At the very least it should minimise pain for you if you move it during the night.'

He didn't argue—well, not about the ankle—because he'd remembered where her tirade had begun.

'A misogynistic medico? What gives you the impression of misogynism—if there is such a word?'

He heard her chuckle.

'I thought you might have missed that bit,' she told him, binding his ankle with such professional skill he didn't feel any additional pain. 'But I did pick up certain vibes during lunch—comments on women in general, and a few directed at particular women among the guests. I think you accused me earlier in the day of bitchiness—or perhaps I accused myself—but some of the remarks emanating from your lips would have beaten anything I might have said hands down.'

Cal tried to think back, but the immediate past seemed lost somewhere in the haze of pain his injuries were causing. Though given his general attitude from the moment Mount Spec had been proposed as a wedding venue, he wasn't surprised.

What did surprise him was the strength of his reaction to her words. He didn't want Blythe judging him by his behaviour at the lunch.

'It's always hard, going back to the property,' he told her, then realised he was making excuses which made him sound even weaker.

'Especially hard, I imagine, to a wedding.'

Her comment surprised him and he peered towards where she'd settled by the fire when she'd finished binding his ankle. He hadn't heard any sarcasm in her voice, but he wasn't good at the nuances of female conversation anyway. Marriage to Grace had taught him that much.

'Yes!' he said, because the words seemed to hang in the air between them, needing some acknowledgement or closure.

'So why did you go?'

Cal shrugged, then winced as the movement caused pain.

'I suppose because Lileth's a cousin. Although we hadn't seen anything of each other since we were children, she cared enough to come out to meet me again. And Mark's become a friend as well as a colleague, though when I agreed to be best man, the wedding was going to be held at Lileth's home—your mother's home.'

'Well, at least I wasn't the only one put out by the all-powerful grandfather decreeing she be married on the property!'

Blythe sounded placated, but her words prompted a memory of Cal's final conversation with his grandfather, just before leaving Mount Spec.

'He's not so all-powerful these days,' he said, speaking slowly as he put some vague impressions into words. 'If anything, he's suddenly very much aware of his own mortality. I think wanting to have Lileth marry up there was his way of making amends.'

'And you? Did he make his peace with you?'

Again Cal peered towards his companion, wanting to see her face as she plucked these too-perceptive questions and comments out of thin air. But all he could see was firelight gleaming on her hair and the outline of her profile against the light.

'What makes you think it was necessary?' he asked, and saw her shoulders move as she laughed.

'You were the heir—the first-born grandson—and, no matter what you say, someone of your grandfather's vintage would put stock in primogeniture. And for some reason, you turn your back on your heritage and go off to the city to study medicine. He must have been horrified—perhaps even devastated.'

Cal couldn't deny either the horror or the devastation, so said nothing, though his mind returned to those lonely nights when he'd first been in the city—so adrift from all that was familiar.

'Why?'

The softly spoken air drifted across the night air and settled in his head but, though he knew what she was asking, answering wasn't easy.

'You obviously have that deep, inbred love for the country, so why leave the family farm—if one can describe such a vast spread in that way—to be a doctor?'

Blythe had no sooner uttered the words than she wished them unspoken. Of all the stupid, insensitive things to blurt out! She reached out to rest her hand lightly on his knee.

'I'm sorry! Of course you couldn't have stayed on at the property once your wife had taken up with your brother. It must have been agonising for you. I imagine getting away was all you could think of...' She stopped as her thoughts hit a snag. 'Though why you'd choose medicine as an escape unless you're an absolute glutton for punishment, I don't know. I would have thought there were dozens of easier options—things connected with the land, a stock and station agent...'

Not knowing much about country life, she ran out of suggestions, but she'd felt Cal's reaction to her hand on his knee and withdrew it hurriedly.

'You've turned all womanly again,' he growled, coolness back in his deep voice. 'Imagining me bereft and broken-hearted.'

Blythe peered at him, but the firelight revealed little emotion on his face.

'I didn't mention broken-hearted,' she muttered at him, obscurely upset by the 'womanly' jibe. 'But surely, particularly in such a close community, you must have been at least slightly peeved to have your wife go off with your brother.'

'That's pure speculation on your part—my wife "going off", as you succinctly put it, with my brother. For all you know, it could have been my decision to leave and follow up on a lifelong interest in medicine.'

'Was it?'

He didn't answer immediately and a quick glance his way showed only his profile, as he, too, gazed into the flames.

'I *was* interested in improving medical facilities in the country and I'd been on a national committee which was looking into the provision of rural medical services for a couple of years. I'm three years older than Chris, but when he was old enough and experienced enough to know running Mount Spec was what *he* wanted to do, I was free to do as I wished. I decided I should put my money where my mouth was, so to speak, and actually do something about improving services. To do that, I had to begin by knowing more than I did about doctoring. So I went off to the city to study medicine.'

The story came out so smoothly, Blythe wondered if it had been rehearsed. Or told so often the words were like a mantra. But there were holes big enough to drown in and she was too curious for subtlety, so she leapt into the biggest of them. 'You said *you* were free. If she hadn't taken up with your brother by then, why didn't Grace go with you?'

She was watching the dark shadow of his body so saw his shoulders move in a shrug, then the wince of pain as his injury objected.

'Grace found she liked Mount Spec more than she liked me.' The harshness in his voice suggested remembered pain, for all his denial of heartbreak, but after his previous putdown Blythe knew better than to offer sympathy. 'Our marriage had been more or less preordained by both our families. It was never a grand passion, and Grace was entitled to do as she wished, which was to remain as chatelaine of Mount Spec.'

'Well, of all the selfish, grasping attitudes!' Blythe blurted out as indignation overcame her desire to remain unmoved by his story.

He turned to face her, and in the firelight she could see his eyebrows tugged closer in a frown.

'Do you think so? Grace and I married young, but my experience of women since suggests they're far more pragmatic than men give them credit for. Women go for the practical in decision-making—the emotional trip is just a cover-up.'

'I knew you were a misogynist,' Blythe muttered darkly, then heard his chuckle warm the darkness between them.

'No way, merely a realist. I mean, look at Mark and Lileth. Mark was perfectly happy practising at Creamunna but even you don't believe Lileth will last long in the country. So what will happen? Mark will move somewhere else. It's the woman who influences most decisions in marriages.'

'Though not in your case,' Blythe pointed out, as anger at his attitude began to fire her blood. 'You proved your own snide theory wrong. You simply abandoned your wife and family to go off and do what you wanted to do. And you make out women are the selfish ones! If you'd been influenced by your wife, you'd have stayed.'

'In a household with a cook, a housekeeper, several other helpers, not to mention a nanny and a governess, my wife and family were hardly abandoned,' he retorted coldly.

Blythe shook her head. Experience had taught her it was impossible to understand other people's relationships, but this man's cold appraisal of his marriage break-up was so far beyond her comprehension it was unbelievable.

Something akin to disappointment fluttered in her chest and she had to remind herself that once she was on the bus she'd never see him again, so what did it matter how Cal viewed women or relationships?

Thinking of the bus reminded her of an earlier, unanswered question.

'Where will the helicopter take us?'

If he was surprised by the conversational switch, he didn't show it, merely glancing her way before saying, 'Derryville, I imagine. From there it's a two-hour drive to Creamunna, but you can get the bus from Derryville.'

The dismissal in his words was unmistakable. So blunt, in fact, Blythe reacted before thinking.

'Good riddance to bad rubbish, in fact!' she snapped. 'And what about you? I suppose you're intending to do the martyr thing. Get patched up in the bigger town then hobble back to work, bravely holding the fort until Mark gets back. Fat lot of good you'll be to the patients!'

She'd expected him to match her rudeness, perhaps demanding to know what business it was of hers anyway, but he said nothing, the silence in the end seeming so loud she had to break it.

If only she could think of something to say...

'Actually—' Cal beat her to it '—I've been thinking about that. You say you're a doctor. Your job in the UK has fallen through. You've spent money you could ill afford flying up to the wedding. You're on the spot—or almost on the spot. How about it?'

Blythe hesitated. She'd been so busy thinking up a cutting remark to answer his 'you say you're a doctor', she'd almost missed the rest. And now, though she'd pieced it together in her head, it still didn't seem to make sense.

'After all, given your propensity to bring disaster down on people's heads, it could even be seen as a way to make amends,' he added, and she guessed from his tone of voice he was smiling as he spoke.

Pleased with himself, no doubt!

Smug!

'You told me it was dirt in the fuel, not me, that caused your problem, so don't try the guilt trip. The answer's no, no way, not in a hundred years.'

'What about a "please, Blythe"? Didn't you tell me that worked for your mother?'

'We'll leave my mother out of this.'

'Then what about your Hippocratic oath? Aren't you sworn to give help where it's needed? For the next few weeks—six, in fact, if you'd be willing to stay until Mark returns—it's most definitely going to be needed in Creamunna.'

He must be out of his mind, Cal decided. Not only suggesting this woman work with him, but practically begging her to stay. Although, if he could get over this physical attraction thing, it was a sensible idea. And the attraction *was* only physical! She was so scratchy, and defensive, and obviously scornful of men, she was the last kind of woman with whom he'd want to share a relationship.

'I don't think the Hippocratic oath mentioned Creamunna,' she snapped, but the snap lacked bite and he sensed her weakening.

'I'd pay well. The practice can afford it. Even if you could give me a couple of weeks—by then my shoulder and ankle will both be a lot better and I'll be used to getting around with a stick. Please, Blythe—it's for the townspeople, not me. They don't deserve to be left with only a broken-down crock to provide services for them.'

I must be out of my mind to even be considering it, Blythe thought, but she had just over six weeks before her altered departure date, and she'd need to do something or go mad. She'd already been considering finding locum work to replenish the coffers...

'Free board? Mark and I share a big house, tons of room, and we have a housekeeper who's an inspired cook, so you wouldn't have any extra duties at all. Just see to patients. I can sit in on consultations if you like so you won't even have to study all their histories.'

He was stating facts, not pleading, yet Blythe could feel his persistence getting under her skin—the way his voice did, in fact—setting up strange flickering sensations in her nerves.

'Let me think about it,' she said, mainly to stop him talking.

'When a parent says that to child, it usually means no,' he said. 'Why not? A hot date back in Brisbane? Some man waiting impatiently for your return? Or is it simply that you don't like the country? Can't take the dust and flies?'

Now the flickering sensations were in her blood, and they were fired by rage, not awareness.

'Hot date indeed! Can't take the dust and flies!' She spat the words at him. 'For someone asking a favour, you're being extremely rude!'

Cal's chuckle surprised her.

'Well, sweet talking obviously wasn't going to work, so I had to try something different. I thought the dust and flies jibe might get you.' He paused, and she knew he'd turned to look at her. 'But you're an attractive enough woman. It was reasonable to suppose there was a man waiting for you somewhere. Is he in London? Is that the reason for the trip?'

Blythe was so distracted by this presumption—and so put out by the 'attractive enough' remark—she forgot what they'd been arguing about in the first place.

'Why do men always assume a woman is incomplete without a man? As for thinking I'd go rushing off to London because of one, I like your cheek. Especially when your wife showed no inclination to go rushing off after you to Brisbane, or wherever it was you went to study!'

'My ex-wife,' he said, in a voice so cold Blythe shivered.

She stared into the flames, wondering why her remark had so effectively killed the conversation—such as it was. OK, so it had been a rude thing to say, but he'd been equally rude, and there'd been a casualness about their sparring that had lightened even the remarks to which she'd objected.

But obviously his wife's defection had cut deeper than he made out, and while he could speak unemotionally, even jokingly of it, he couldn't handle others bringing up the subject.

Blue light flickered close to the heart of the fire, and with her eyes mesmerised by its dance and the cold night closing around her, she felt a sudden wave of pity for the man sweep over her and heard a voice which sounded remarkably like her own say, 'I suppose I could give you a couple of weeks.'

CHAPTER FIVE

'THANKS.'

Cal knew he should say more—express his gratitude more whole-heartedly—but while his professional self was relieved he'd found someone to share his workload, his personal self was less sure this was a good idea.

He glanced her way. Blythe's head was bent towards the fire and the glow fed a pink translucence into the skin on the cheek he could see. Her hair was a dark cloud, lit here and there, when the flames flickered, with gold. She was a beautiful, intelligent woman...

'*Why* is there no man in your life?'

Knew it was the wrong question the moment it slipped out. She'd already ripped shreds off him for suggesting there might be one, so to probe as to the absence...

Dumb, dumb, dumb!

But though he'd expected a dressing-down—or some kind of angry retort—he received instead a smile.

'It must be because I'm hungry I haven't thrown the fire at you,' she said. 'Or perhaps the isolation makes personal questions seem OK.'

She thrust her hand through her hair, pushing it back from her face, the long fingers combing it backwards so he saw her whole profile instead of just one pink-flushed cheek.

'I was off men for a while, but recently I've decided on a whole new approach to the male-female thing.' She turned so she was facing him and, though he couldn't see it, he knew she must be grinning, for mischievous delight filtered into her voice as she continued.

'I've decided to go for the practical approach. I'm a woman, I enjoy the company of men, and I—' She stopped abruptly, looking up to the sky as if inspiration might come from on high.

Then she looked back at him and finished what she'd been saying in a voice that dared him to comment.

'I like…sex. We're both adults here and there's no other way to say it that doesn't sound twee or prudish. I'm not saying I'm a sex maniac, or that I can't do without it, but I've come to the conclusion that men have had this sex thing worked out better than women for years. They meet a woman to whom they're attracted and the first thing that pops into their head is how they can get her into the cot. They begin a campaign with that end in mind.'

She turned away to stir the fire, sending a bright shower of sparks into the air.

'Women, generally speaking, though things are changing now, start from some inbred position where they connect sex with love and love with marriage so they get tangled up right from the start because they're working on a different campaign. By the time they get to bed with the guy, they're thinking relationship whereas he's thinking satisfaction.'

It was a strange conversation to be having in the middle of nowhere, but Cal had seen rough bushmen turn to poets by a campfire at night, so he wasn't altogether surprised. Though the content was certainly different to the conversations at a mustering camp…

'So, you're going for satisfaction instead of relationships from now on? Is that what you're saying?'

Blythe tilted a defiant chin in his direction.

'Yes, it is. In fact, after you and I had talked a bit and you'd made me laugh—I can't remember why, something stupid I guess—I thought you might have been a good candidate for a trial run. Whatever chemical it is that jump-starts physical attraction had kicked in and we danced well together and that's a physical thing, isn't it?'

She stopped as if she'd finished the conversation, leaving Cal stuck out on a limb.

And very put out!

'And?' he prompted.

'And what?'

'And what happened then? Were you still considering me for the guinea pig when we crashed? Is it because I'm injured you've decided I wouldn't do? I'm sure once I'm patched up, an inventive woman like you could think of some way to conduct your experiment.'

'Don't take it so personally,' she retorted, then she chuckled and reached out to touch him lightly on his good shoulder. 'Actually, that was a really good remark, wasn't it? That's exactly the kind of thing men say to women when they're edging away from relationship situations. But in your case, it wasn't the injury—I'd crossed you off before that. Neither was it anything against you. It just seemed a bit crass to start with someone who's more or less related. I mean, if we end up at a family christening together some time in the future, and you've remarried, it might be awkward.'

'I didn't think a woman who wore a curtain to a wedding would know the meaning of awkward,' Cal snapped, then instantly regretted it as she bowed her head and poked unnecessarily at the fire.

He'd glimpsed her vulnerability before, but she cloaked it so well with bravado he tended to forget about it.

'I'm sorry—that was a low blow. Blame it on perversity. I was hitting back because there was some part of me that reacted badly to being taken out of your calculations. Probably the part of me that was attracted to you right from the start. It's a funny thing, attraction, isn't it?'

She lifted her head and because she'd made the fire flare up with her poking, he saw her smile.

'Really weird,' she agreed. 'But no weirder than this conversation. I've said things to you, a stranger, that I wouldn't say to my best friend. I mean, I've thought this stuff about relationships and all, but that's as far as I've got. Now suddenly I'm talking to you about chemistry and sex.'

'And suggesting we're practically related, which we're not, and marrying me off again, which isn't going to happen. I mean, I've got two kids, so there's no real reason to remarry.'

'Because you've been there and done that—we keep coming back to that phrase, don't we?'

Cal thought for a moment, then, perhaps because he sensed he'd hurt her earlier, or perhaps because she'd been so open and honest herself, he found himself telling her the truth.

'I think if the first experience is good, a man would be happy to repeat marriage, but I watched my wife fall in love with my brother—really fall in love in a way she never had with me. Sheer self-preservation makes me tell the story differently, but what you assumed had happened did happen, Blythe…'

'Wounding you in such a way thick scars have grown around your heart?' she finished for him. 'Been there, too. Perhaps we should start abbreviating like we do on emails and text messages. BTDT, we can say to each other.'

Then she leant forward from where she was now kneeling by the fire, and kissed him carefully, but very firmly on the lips, before drawing away and looking up at the sky.

'Moon madness, do you think?'

'There's no moon,' Cal said quietly.

'No moon, but a gazillion stars,' Blythe said, as she took

in the wide arc of the heavens—the stars lighting the night like diamanté scattered on black velvet.

Her heart ached for this man who had suffered what must be the ultimate betrayal. What she'd been through had been minor in comparison. But wanting to weep for him was no help, and there was no way she could rewrite the past.

But she could at least try to make him as comfortable as possible for tonight. If she concentrated on practical matters...

'You should try to sleep.'

She reached out for her bag and held it open towards the fire so she could find the tablets she had. She was glad it was dark, so Cal couldn't see the emotion she knew would be showing in her cheeks. It had been bad enough telling the man she fancied him as a sex object, but then to have her guess about his marriage confirmed...

'You were out of it for a while and, though it's probably only mild concussion, you should still rest.'

She hoped she sounded cooler than she felt.

Her fingers found the crumpled blister pack and she pushed out two tablets, poured water into the vitamin container and edged closer to hand him first the tablets then the drink.

'Better have another drink,' she told him, wriggling backwards again. Touching his hand as she'd passed him the water had been enough to tell her that, although her mind had rejected Cal, the chemistry was still at work.

But given the overall situation, she'd better learn to ignore it.

'Now, you'll be best off lying on your left side. Can you wriggle around so you're facing the fire? Then I can lie behind you to keep your back warm.'

'And what will keep your back warm?'

Blythe grinned at him.

'Mortification most probably. I still can't believe I told you all the things I did.'

'I'm honoured,' Cal said, though Blythe guessed he didn't mean it. She'd probably just confirmed his not-so-high opinion of women.

He was shifting his position by pulling himself along the ground with his good foot—coming closer, which caused apprehension where embarrassment had been.

'But you've got it wrong about the way to sleep. I'd be happy for you to keep my back warm, but you should be the one near the fire. I'll lie here so you can curl around me, and your back will be warmed by the fire.'

'What about your front? You're the injured one. The one who should be kept warm.'

He smiled at her.

'Believe me, I'll be warm,' he said, and heat, not from mortification, shimmied through Blythe's body.

Get your mind off sex, she ordered herself, standing up and moving away with a muttered excuse she hoped he'd take for a personal need. Though, thinking of that, she should use the time—and give him time and space for whatever he might need to do.

Eventually, they settled down on the hard ground, sharing the coat which he'd opened and spread by the fire and covered by his dinner jacket and the remnants of the curtain. Blythe felt Cal's warmth feed into her body, while her nose, pressed close to his neck so they could share his bag as a pillow, drew in the man smell of him.

Yet, in spite of his nearness all around her, the night pressed close, the silence so complete it almost echoed. And into her heart crept all the doubt and fear talking had kept at bay earlier.

'I'm glad we're snuggling,' she whispered, when a muttered curse told her he was still awake and, no doubt, hurting. 'The world seems so much bigger out here. All the nothingness makes two humans seem very, very small and totally insignificant in the grand scheme of things. I guess I feel as lost out here as you did in the city.'

She'd tried to make it sound like she was joking, but the quaver in her voice sounded more like pathos than laughter.

'Damn this shoulder,' Cal said, shifting then wincing, so she moved before he could bump against her. 'I should be holding you, not the other way around. Offering you comfort and protection—and not because you're a woman and I think you need protection. Or because of the chemistry you mentioned earlier. But because this is my environment.'

He rolled over onto his back and reached out for her with his good hand.

'Look, my shoulder is aching like hell whichever way I lie, so I'll stay on my back and you come and cuddle up to my good side. Let me hold you, Blythe. That's the least I can do.'

It sounded great—definitely the best offer she'd had for some time. She scuttled around him, carrying the dinner jacket and curtain, then settled herself down beside him, chin resting on his good shoulder, his arm holding her close.

'Now I'll tell you stories,' he said, and the deep mellow voice, telling her about campfires and musters and the sound of cattle lowing in the night, eased all her fears and soothed her into sleep.

Help arrived with the dawn. First in the guise of a laconic farmer.

'Missus thought you might like a hot drink and a bit of tucker,' he announced, climbing out the cab of his ute and pausing briefly to lift a box from the tray back before heading towards them.

'Soon as I saw you both sit up I radioed the missus to call the rescue service and tell 'em I'd found you.'

He deposited the box on the ground in front of them and held out his hand.

'Ted Cummins, Careela.'

'I'm Cal Whitworth, Ted, and this is Blythe Jones, and your missus was right—I'd kill for a hot drink.'

Ted nodded to Blythe and began to unpack the box, setting out a Thermos and cups then delving in again, producing sandwiches that smelt as if they'd been made with newly baked bread.

'I'm so hungry I'd have eaten a rag doll,' Blythe said, accepting a sandwich and nodding yes to coffee. 'But these are delicious. Does your wife make her own bread?'

'Have to make your own everything, just about, out here,' Ted told her. 'Easier these days with electricity and fancy machines. When my mother first came here, Dad built a roof to shelter them from the sun and keep the bed and provisions under, and Mum cooked over an open fire. When the rains came, they hung tarpaulins down the rainy side to stop it blowing in.'

He nodded towards Cal.

'Though the real pioneers were the women like the doc here's great-grandmother. She's part of history, she is. One of the first white women in the Northern Territory.'

Blythe stopped eating long enough to smile at Cal.

'Lileth's great-grandmother?' she said, and saw his eyes light up as he appreciated the joke.

But he nodded to Ted, then explained, 'But for all her hardships, she lived until she was nearly ninety. Said it was hard work kept her going. I remember, as a child, listening to her stories. Her biggest regret, she used to say, was when the bullock wagon bogged after an unexpected downpour. Apparently, my grandfather needed something to put under the wheels of the wagon so the bullocks could pull it free, and he chose what he considered the least necessary items they were carrying. These happened to be several sets of silver cutlery his wife had been given as part of her trousseau. They were packed in solid wooden cases—things like cake forks and carving sets as well as normal cutlery.'

Ted was already laughing but Blythe failed to get the joke.

'So what happened?' she demanded.

'Oh, they were just right for the job. The wheels caught on them and came free, my great-grandfather led the bullocks onto less treacherous ground, and that was that.'

'He *did* go back for the cutlery, didn't he?'

'No way he could.' Ted answered for Cal. 'Once he had those wheels moving he wouldn't have wanted to stop and bog down again. Besides, that black soil when it's wet— it'd swallow a bullock in no time flat. He'd never have found those boxes.'

A clattering noise, at first far off but coming steadily closer, stopped the conversation. Blythe finished her coffee and took another sandwich, while Ted hurried over to his ute and brought out a roll of bright blue plastic.

'He'll spread it so the pilot can see where to land,' Cal explained. 'In most places, you'd spread something white, but against the salt it might not stand out, so blue's good.'

'And people have the right colour plastic hanging about their houses, ready to spread should an emergency arise?' Blythe shook her head. 'That's harder to believe than your ancestor leaving his wife's silver cutlery behind.'

Cal chuckled.

'Ted probably has a dozen uses for the plastic,' he said. 'Lining feed bins, keeping rain off an injured animal, or off himself if he's working on a borehole pump in the wet season.'

'I don't even know what a borehole pump is!' Blythe muttered, but the helicopter was coming down and the words were drowned out by the noise it made.

CHAPTER SIX

ONE week later, Blythe lay on the deck by the small, above-ground pool in the back yard of the 'Doctor's House', as the rambling old wooden building was known.

Sunday was the doctors' official day off—no surgery and no hospital round unless requested by staff. She was on call for emergencies but Cal had assured her the locals tried hard not to have emergencies on Sundays.

She could, had she wanted, have taken herself off to Derryville, but she'd seen Derryville the previous Sunday when the rescue helicopter had deposited her and Cal at the hospital there, and, though a larger town than Creamunna, it shut down on the Sabbath just as comprehensively.

Though the hospital staff there had been wonderful, fussing over Cal as X-rays had confirmed the broken clavicle but ruled out a broken ankle—badly sprained was the hospital doctor's opinion.

So, she was lying by the pool and wishing for company. Any company, even Mrs Robertson, with her interminable chatter about people Blythe didn't know, would have done. She knew better than to hope for Cal's company. Within twenty-four hours of arriving in the place, she'd realised he was a workaholic and, though not able to do much doctoring, he would sit at the computer for hours on end.

Catching up, he said, but on what, he didn't say.

In fact, he didn't say much at all. Ever.

He'd sat in on her initial consultations, but after the first morning, which had been awkward for both doctors and the patient, he'd left her on her own.

93

Actually, now she thought about it, a little praise wouldn't have hurt…

'You'll get burnt if you lie there for longer than half an hour.'

'So?' Blythe snapped, forgetting she'd been wanting company and lifting her head to glare at it now it had arrived.

'So then we'd have two crocks for doctors. Not fair on the patients.'

'Bugger the patients,' Blythe muttered, but she rolled over to expose her front side to the sun, knowing the man was, as annoyingly as ever, right.

She closed her eyes to shut out the sun, and assumed Cal had walked away—back to the computer, no doubt— so was startled when she heard a chair creak as if weight was being lowered into it.

'What don't you like about the town?' Cal asked, and she had to open one eye so she could squint at him.

'What do you mean, what don't I like about the town? Did I say I didn't like the town? What gives you the right to make these assumptions?'

'A little tetchy today, are we? Too much wine last night?'

Blythe closed the eye again, and bit back a groan.

She had had too much wine the previous night, but Cal's suggestion that he open a bottle to have with their dinner had made her feel as if it had been a special occasion. Then she'd realised that thinking of 'special occasion' and 'Cal' in the same sentence wasn't good, so she'd gulped instead of sipped.

'I didn't mean it that way—that you didn't like the town.' He must have realised she wasn't going to answer him. 'I know it's only been a week, but I'd really like to know how you feel about your introduction to rural medicine. What made it hard? What might have made it easier?'

You being here.

You not being here.

Blythe's head supplied the answers to his questions, but she didn't pass them on. The man was egotistical enough—it came through in the assured way he moved, even with a walking stick, in the way he spoke, in his certainty about things. And a week of seeing disappointment on the faces of women when they'd realised Blythe was to be their doctor confirmed her guess that the women of Creamunna had added to his ego problem rather than detracted from it.

She closed her eyes more tightly as she silently acknowledged her outrageous conversation by the fire the previous week would probably have inflated it as well, then tried to blank the memory out again.

She spent a lot of her time at Creamunna doing that— blanking out memories. Of conversations. Of how she'd felt, lying with his arm around her while he'd told her stories...

'It's important to know,' he persisted, breaking into her straying and as yet unblanked-out thoughts. 'Of course, it would have been better if you were my wife—that's really the perspective I need to get—but a woman doctor—that's good too.'

Blythe gave up ignoring him—and the blanking business. She sat up and turned to face him, adjusting the top of the quite classy black bikini she'd been surprised to find in Creamunna's one and only clothing store.

'It'd be better if I were your wife? What are we talking about here, Dr Whitworth? Your wife?'

Her voice had got a bit shrill by the last bit of her contribution to the conversation, but what could you expect?

'It's nothing personal,' he said, looking not at her but

across the back yard to where a couple of rainbow lorikeets were picking up grass seed. 'I think I told you I'm interested in rural medicine and in encouraging medical personnel to work in rural areas. This began before I became a doctor, but the interest has continued. It's really why I'm at Creamunna. I need to experience rural practice in order to understand how to make it more attractive to potential employees. So a wife's perspective would have been handy. Maybe Lileth will come and even if she only stays a short time, I could ask her.'

'And do what with the information?'

Blythe's reply was so abrupt Cal was forced to look back at her, though he'd been trying not to since his earlier sighting of all the creamy skin not covered by the black bikini had alerted his libido to its recent lack of action.

Throwing a blanket over her would help, but it would be hard to explain such an action.

If only she hadn't suggested she'd been interested in him—purely for sex, of course...

He focussed on his work.

'I'm compiling data. Actually, I'm not the only one—there are other members of the rural medicine committee who are also looking into this. Then, once we have a reasonably large survey group, we can look at the answers and if we identify a problem, we see what we can do to remedy it.'

Blythe frowned at him as if his explanation lacked something so he launched into an example.

'Take shopping. In an early survey, access to department stores was one of the things women really missed when they came out here. The committee liased with a couple of big firms and women can now shop on-line.'

'Wow! Trying on a dress on-line—that would be interesting.'

At times like this, when she made him want to grind his

teeth, Cal wondered why he'd persuaded her to stay! But he bit back his own caustic comment, and continued.

'It's not ideal, but it's better than nothing. The problem then was that a lot of people weren't internet savvy, so the committee organised a technology support person to travel around, giving lessons in everything from basic computer skills to setting up your own website.'

'That's good, practical help,' his guest admitted. 'I'm not a shopaholic myself and I was amazed at the range of clothes I found in Mrs Warburton's emporium, but I can understand some people might like more options.'

She paused then smiled at him—the cheeky, luminous grin she gave because she must know it infuriated him.

Or his reaction to it infuriated him...

'You'll notice I said "people", not "women". I know men who spend more time in shops than most of the women I know. A male shopaholic is far worse than the female of the species.'

Cal shrugged. He didn't know how it happened, but he was always getting into this kind of conversation with Blythe—as if they couldn't talk without arguing over something.

'I'm not normally an argumentative person,' he complained, then realised he was continuing his thoughts, not the conversation.

And she was grinning at him again, as if she knew exactly what he'd been thinking.

The phone saved him from further embarrassment, Blythe lifting the handpiece from beside where she sat and answering it with a cool, 'Blythe Jones speaking.'

'Yes. Yes?'

She cocked her eyebrows enquiringly at Cal.

'Yes, OK, we'll be there.'

She thumbed the button to end the call, then said, 'Buck-jumping at a place called Whitestone? Ring any bells?'

'Oh hell, I'd forgotten all about it. What time?'

'Two-thirty. How far away is it?'

'Less than an hour. We'll make it.'

'Just!' Blythe was already on her feet and heading towards the house.

'You don't have to come,' Cal called after her. 'The ambulance will be there, and I can drive so I'll go out and can give advice if it's needed.'

'I guess you could drive at a pinch but you'd be a danger to yourself and all other road-users,' she said, swinging back to give him a genuine smile. 'Anyway, I've never seen buck-jumping. I don't even know what it is, but if it's part of the country experience, then I'm in.'

She hurried off, reappearing in an incredibly short time, the creamy skin demurely covered in jeans and a brightly embroidered top that looked like something women in Eastern Europe might wear as part of a national costume.

'I like the way you country folk give distances in time,' she said, lifting the car keys from the hook and heading out the door, leaving him to hobble after her as best he could. 'I didn't understand it until I went out to Mr Crichton's on Thursday. Though it can't be more than thirty k's, the road's so bad once you leave the bitumen, it took an hour.'

Cal frowned at the bottom swaying seductively along in front of him. She'd been virtually dragooned into helping out for a few weeks, and, though she argued non-stop with him, she seemed to find everything else in the 'country experience' fascinating and absorbing and delightfully interesting. She was obviously the wrong person to have asked about what she didn't like...

'Here, you slide in and I'll take your stick.'

She was holding the car door open for him now and, though he hated to be so dependent on anyone, he had to admit she did things like this with a minimum of fuss.

Maybe she knew his frustration levels—with the injuries, not libido this time, though there was that as well—were so high, any unnecessary fussing might have driven him to violence.

'We go out along the Western Highway,' he told her, as she backed the car competently out through the front gate.

'So, tell me more about the rural medicine committee,' she suggested, when they were low-flying along the deserted highway.

Cal, always nervous when someone else was driving, leaned across to check the speedometer.

'Only five k's over the limit,' his chauffeur assured him. 'Stop panicking.'

But he felt the slowing as she lifted her foot—marginally, he guessed—off the accelerator.

'There are government agencies and organisations involved in encouraging doctors to practise in isolated areas, but this committee is more a practical thing, made up of people both inside and outside medicine with an interest in making sure there are services on the ground.'

'People like you were when you first became involved— back when you were a cattle baron, not a doctor.'

'Hardly a baron,' Cal corrected dryly, 'but, yes, people like me, as well as doctors, nurses and therapists who have worked, or are still working, in rural communities.'

Blythe nodded her understanding, wondering again about this man's past and the journey that had led him to the strong commitment he obviously had to rural medicine.

She considered asking, but guessed he'd fob her off, as he did whenever her questions verged towards the personal, so she asked about buck-jumping instead because, given the strange tension that always seemed to stretch between them when they were together, not talking wasn't an option.

'Been to a rodeo?'

He often answered her question with a question, a little habit that now made her smile.

'Not a lot of them happening down in the city,' she reminded him. 'But I know about them. Foolish youth ride wild bulls—isn't that the idea?'

'Partly,' he agreed, 'though they're not all youths and certainly not foolish. It's sport that takes a lot of stamina as well as guts.'

'Spilling everywhere no doubt.'

Cal chuckled, the sound causing pleasant tremors on Blythe's skin and a spurt of satisfaction in her mind. He laughed so rarely she now treated making him laugh as a challenge, giving herself a mental pat on the back when she succeeded.

'Buck-jumping is part of most rodeos. It's done on horses, not bulls, and as well as being included in rodeos, there's a buck-jumping circuit as well. Most weekends there'll be a buck-jumping competition somewhere, and riders and horses travel to compete.'

'The horses travel to compete? Do people try to get bucked off their own horses?'

A smile this time—no pat on the back for it, though, as it was his condescending 'poor city girl' type of smile.

'The horses are kept especially for buck-jumping. A good bucker is worth big money, because everyone wants to ride him.'

'Everyone wants to ride him?' Blythe repeated. Forget condescending smiles, she *was* a city girl and way out of her depth here. 'If I had to ride a bucking horse, I'd far rather have one without a buck left in him—or maybe one little buck, just for show.'

Another smile, this one more genuine than the first.

'The riders score points,' Cal explained, 'firstly for staying on the required time, and secondly for how well they ride. That depends on how well the horse bucks. If it ambles out and pig-roots a couple of times, it's not much of a ride so you don't get a good score, which is why all the riders want a good horse—one that will buck the hell out of them.'

'I am going to assume this is a male thing—beyond the comprehension of female minds,' Blythe muttered, but was swiftly corrected.

'No way. You get women riders as well. There'll be at least two out at Whitestone today.' Alerted by something in his voice, she glanced his way and caught the twinkle in the eyes that were watching and waiting for her reaction. 'In fact, you know one of them. Janet Speares.'

'Janet Speares, the Director of Nursing at the hospital?' No wonder he'd been alert for her reaction! 'She rides wild horses that try to buck her off?'

'She does, and does it well. In fact, she was the women's buck-jumping champ at Derryville Rodeo this year.'

Blythe concentrated on driving while she took this in. Janet Speares was a slim, lithe slip of a woman in her late twenties, always immaculately groomed. Imagining her bouncing around on the top of a bucking horse was impossible.

Blythe glanced at her companion again, sure he must be pulling her leg, but he looked quite serious.

Whitestone turned out to be a cattle property, not another small town, and, as they turned off the bitumen onto the drive that led to the homestead, clouds of dust rose and swirled behind them.

'Bit dry out here. Means it will be dusty,' Cal remarked, and though Blythe decided he must be more relaxed than usual as he rarely made that kind of purely conversational remark, she didn't think more about it.

Until the first horse and rider came out of the chute, and

as the horse bucked, the dust in the makeshift ring rose in spiralling clouds. Fine as talcum powder, it hung in the air, insinuated itself into nostrils and settled on skin and clothing. Within minutes everyone had the same brown dusty-all-over look.

'At the bigger rodeos they have a water truck that waters the ground a few times in between events, so the dust settles,' Cal explained, but as Janet Speares was, at that moment, being thrown awkwardly through the air, Blythe couldn't answer.

She started from her seat, sure the woman must be badly injured, but Cal pulled her back.

'She's OK, and even if she wasn't, the ambos would look at her first. They know we're here if we're needed, but don't fuss. Rough riders and buck-jumpers hate people to think that they're injured. I've seen a fellow with a broken pelvis walk out of the ring.'

But the next rider wasn't as lucky. Thrown off before the horse was properly in the ring, the young man was slow to roll away, and before the horse-mounted steward whose job it was to grab the horse's halter and release the surcingle could grab the bucking animal, it had come down on top of the rider, lethal hooves plummeting into his abdomen.

'This time we go,' Blythe said, and Cal didn't argue, following more slowly as she dashed around the ring towards the gate where ambulance officers were already jogging through.

The young rider was curled up on the ground, his hands clenched and arms crossed protectively across his stomach.

'Let's have a look at you, mate,' the older of the two attendants said, but the more he tried to ease the lad into a prone position, the tighter the legs curled.

'He's moving his limbs, which suggests there's no spinal damage, so could we get him out of the dust?' Blythe suggested.

'It's my shoulder, my left shoulder,' the lad said, but Blythe was more worried about what damage the horse's hooves might have done.

One of the attendants left, returning seconds later with a light stretcher. By this time Cal had arrived, and it was he who supervised lifting the young man onto the stretcher.

Blythe helped carry it towards the ambulance where they lowered the stretcher onto the collapsible frame of the trolley. The bright light from the cabin revealed the lad's ashen face and the blue tinge around his lips. His pulse was fast and unsteady and he gulped at the air with a desperation that frightened Blythe.

One of the ambos was talking to him, asking questions—name, age, any allergies—but the lad was having so much trouble breathing that answering any question was impossible.

'Get an oxygen mask on him right away,' she said, unsnapping studs on the man's fancy shirt and peeling it back to reveal his chest, while the ambo put the mask in place and started the flow of oxygen.

He dragged in a breath of oxygen as she watched but, instead of expanding, the right side of his chest deflated.

'Rib damage, flail chest,' she said, pointing to an area of his rib cage that was already carrying a red hoof mark and was obviously damaged, then glanced up at the ambulance attendant. 'I need an endotracheal tube and a volume-controlled ventilator, or whatever type of ventilator you carry. I'll give him a muscle relaxant if he fights it.'

She took the youth's hand.

'You've broken a couple of ribs and they're pressing on your lungs. I'm going to put a tube down your throat so we can get oxygen into you to stop that damaged lung collapsing. Once the tube's in, we'll give you something for the pain and check out the rest of you.'

Blythe worked steadily, aware of her patient's pain—aware also that he might have other serious injuries but knowing a reliable air supply was the first consideration.

'In A and E we'd call in an anaesthetist to give him a thoracic epidural to stop the pain,' she said, glancing up at Cal when she was satisfied the tube was in place and the ventilator working.

'I can do it—or talk you through it—but we're better tackling it back at the hospital in sterile surroundings. For now make do with local anaesthetic—an intercostal block where the ribs are damaged.'

'Allergies—always the concern of allergic reactions,' Blythe muttered to herself, looking at her patient whom she knew wasn't going to be answering questions any time soon.

'I've brought his contact details and health certificate,' a new voice said, and Blythe turned to find someone she assumed was one of the officials standing at her elbow. 'We get everyone to fill out these forms in case of accident. Who to notify, and so on. I'll call his parents as soon as you know where he's going.'

Blythe passed the information to Cal, who read bits aloud while she injected the mild analgaesic, one ambulance attendant passing her what she needed while the other was checking the patient's blood pressure and, at the same time, keeping a watchful eye on the ventilator.

'His name's Byron Clarke, parents live outside Creamunna. No known allergies, has had tetanus shot recently, and not allergic to penicillin.'

'Well, that's a start,' Blythe said.

'Let's get him to hospital,' Cal suggested, when she began to undo Byron's belt to lower his trousers to check for more damage.

'Blood pressure's low, ninety over sixty.'

'We'll keep an eye on it,' Cal said, then he turned to Blythe. 'Normally, with minor injuries, we'd keep the patient here until the show is over, so there's an ambulance on hand. But this lad needs attention now, so would you ride back to town with him? I'll stay on and the second ambo can drive me back. We shouldn't leave until the show finishes, but if you need me...'

He paused, and Blythe guessed he was worrying about leaving her in charge.

'I'll stay in my car—you can talk to me on the radio. Call me if you have a problem or want to talk about anything at all.'

Blythe nodded, pleased to have Cal sort out the logistics in a situation that was entirely new to her.

'Anything,' he repeated, and touched her lightly on the arm.

The touch made her feel warm and cared-for, so much so she lifted her own hand and rested it on his for a moment.

'I won't let you down,' she promised, and saw his sombre expression lighten as he flashed a smile at her.

'I didn't for a moment think you would. Valkyrie were the handmaidens of the god of war—I'm sure they never let anyone down!' he said.

'Except the people they chose to be slain,' Blythe reminded him.

She waited until the stretcher was secured in place, then climbed in.

''Ware fluids,' Cal said, and she looked at him, smiled and nodded.

Fluid resuscitation was a common emergency response, and a necessity for a patient in shock, but she'd considered the consequences of giving any fluid from the moment she'd seen the uneven chest expansion that was symptomatic of rib and lung damage. Lungs all too easily filled up with fluids, which then became breeding places for all kinds of deadly sepsis. Cal had been right to remind her, in case she hadn't been thinking about it.

Once Byron was in hospital, where he could be monitored, she'd feel easier about giving him fluids, but the BP was a worry. Byron was young—he might always have a low blood pressure. She'd have to take it again, watch for any change in the pulse pressure—the difference between the two numbers. That was a better indication in any change of status.

Strapped into a safety harness beside her patient, she continued her examination, seeing bruising coming out where the second hoof had struck just below the rib cage to the left of the other mark. Possible damage to the diaphragm—and the organs that lay close to it? Spleen and liver. Low BP? Haemorrhage from liver or spleen damage?

What were the percentages?

Her mind, trained to deal with emergencies, asked and answered questions.

Blunt trauma to the upper abdomen or lower thoracic region could cause injury to the spleen in what? Forty-one per cent of cases. Something like that. Liver damage less likely—about twenty per cent possibility. Livers could be repaired, spleens removed, though current thinking was to repair them as well. But in an emergency—to save a life before the patient bled to death—you would remove it. She had good surgical skills, having done extra residency terms in surgery, but an emergency splenectomy in a hospital she barely knew?

She wouldn't think about that just yet.

She felt Byron's hands and knew she'd *have* to think about it. His skin was cold, pale and dry, indicating shock, and his radial pulse so faint she could barely feel it. She squeezed the tip of his forefinger and waited for pinkness to return to the skin. The slowness indicated delayed capillary refill, a symptom of second-phase hypovolaemic shock.

No matter the risk to his lungs, she had to get some fluids into him. The ambulance was travelling smoothly, its springs cushioning the passengers from bumps. This would be easier than cannulations she'd done in helicopters during terms in A and E when she'd been on call for the emergency helicopter in the city. Ambulances were usually set up in the same way, their storage compartments well ordered. She should be able to find all she'd need.

She inflated the blood-pressure cuff around Byron's biceps and was relieved to see a vein come up. As shock progressed, these veins would lie flat, depleted of the blood that kept them healthily rounded.

Ignoring the movement of the ambulance as it shot along the road towards Creamunna, Blythe inserted the cannula, checked the bag of crystalloid solution she'd chosen and connected it up.

Then she watched her patient, but her mind was racing through all the possibilities that lay ahead.

She could probably, at a pinch, do whatever surgery was required, but to perform surgery on a patient whose breathing was already compromised was a tricky business. But she couldn't send a patient on an emergency flight if he was bleeding internally. He might not make the hospital.

And if he was OK to travel, how would a plane flight affect him when his lungs were damaged?

And would it be a plane?

She and Cal had been picked up by a helicopter, but it had been a rescue craft, not an air ambulance. This man would need medical support on any journey.

The questions tumbled in her head as she checked and rechecked the ventilation and the drip.

'Cal Whitworth to EVA 27.'

Cal's voice erupted into the cabin of the ambulance.

'That's us,' the driver said to Blythe, before pressing a button on his radio and replying to Cal.

'Hear you loud and clear, Doc. What's up? Another patient?'

'No, and hopefully there won't be, but could you tell Dr Jones that once she has him stabilised and she's confident he can make the journey, she should call in an air ambulance or the RFDS to fly the patient to Brisbane. We can do a lot of emergency surgery—patching up stuff—on site, but with his lungs compromised, he needs sophisticated support equipment.'

'I was thinking that myself,' Blythe told the driver, who relayed the message to Cal.

The driver radioed ahead to the hospital, explained the situation and asked the nurse on duty to request an urgent emergency airlift for the patient.

She radioed back to them as they reached the edge of town.

'No luck,' she said. 'Sunday afternoon, weekend of traffic accidents, all aircraft are either in service or grounded because the pilots have flown all the allowable hours. Tomorrow morning at the earliest, though they're still checking other options. They might be able to divert a plane this way or find a standby pilot, but emergency services suggest it would be at least three hours before they can get anyone Creamunna. Then it's close to a three-hour flight to Brisbane, plus ambulance transport to the hospital and however long A and E there take to admit him. How does that sound? Do you want to take him on to Derryville? I can call them to send an ambulance to meet you halfway.'

'What do you think?' the driver asked Blythe, who didn't need to think about it. Fluid replacement wasn't helping and the symptoms of shock were becoming more pronounced. The young man needed help now.

'No,' she said, 'but radio Cal, explain the situation and ask him to head back to the hospital right now. He'll have to get someone else to drive him, so he can leave your mate out there in case of another accident. You can drop us off and go straight back out.'

Blythe could feel her knees shaking, but everything she'd ever learnt told her this young man had damaged something in his abdomen that was causing internal bleeding. It wasn't a ruptured aorta, the most disastrous of scenarios, because he'd be in a far more fragile state—or dead—by now, but certainly something else was amiss inside him and, with no specialist on hand to do a laparoscopy, the only way to find out—and fix it—in a hurry was to open him up.

They pulled up at the emergency entrance, doors opening as they arrived and a number of staff coming forward to help.

'I didn't know there were this many people on duty on a Sunday,' Blythe said, as a wardsman and the ambulance attendant detached the stretcher from its anchors then, with the ventilator stashed beneath the patient, slowly lifted the wheeled conveyance out.

'This is Byron Clarke,' she told the staff. 'Rib and lung damage, flail chest, hence the ventilator. He can't talk to us while he's on the ventilator, but we can talk to him, so tell him what you're doing all the time.'

Wanting someone to talk to herself—someone with whom she could share her concerns—she realised for the first time the true isolation of rural medicine. She was it! There *was* no back-up, even for discussion.

Yes, there was! The flying surgeon! Wasn't that what he was there for? Yet even as the thought occurred to her, she knew it was no good. He was based in Roma, more than an hour's flight away, and even supposing she could get hold of him, and he could hustle up his anaesthetist and pilot, *and* they could all come immediately, further delay could be fatal for Byron.

Her frustration with the system was so strong she wanted to rage at someone, but the patient needed her calm and steady, not fuming hysterically. Ah, the hospital had a radio...

'Can you call up Cal on the radio?' she asked one of the nurses. 'Then show me how to talk on it?' She was thinking about peritoneal lavage, a reasonably simple procedure that involved passing warmed sterile fluid through the abdominal cavity then retrieving it to see if there was blood in it.

'Not necessary,' Cal told her when, after explaining the deterioration in Byron's condition and her fear he was going into haemorrhagic shock, she mentioned this to him. 'You'll need to go in. Take him to Theatre and prep him for abdominal surgery. We're only fifteen minutes away. I'll do the anaesthetic.'

'I'm worried about his lungs,' Blythe told him.

'Me, too,' Cal agreed. 'But you've already got a ventilator breathing for him so there shouldn't be a problem. And we can drain his lungs if fluid becomes a problem later. You'll need a nasogastric tube in as well, to decompress his stomach. If you have to take out his spleen, he'll need that post-op. Catheterise him to measure urine output, it's a good guide to circulation. Put in a second large-bore cannula so we're ready if we need to pump more fluid in. Take some blood, type it and make sure you've both resus fluid and plasma on hand. We can't always cross-match blood, but we can give type-specific.'

Blythe handed the mike back to the nurse and headed back to her patient, telling herself this was what medicine was all about. She drew up some blood and took it to do a simple typing test, then ordered what she'd need for Theatre.

As she prepared Byron for Theatre, she told him what was going on, explaining about the operation and how it might be something simple causing the blood loss inside him, but whatever it was, they needed to find it and stop it.

He seemed to understand, nodding from time to time, but Blythe wondered how valid informed consent was when a patient was so ill, in so much pain and under the influence of analgesics.

'Sue Warren's theatre sister, I've called her in,' one of the nurses said.

'And she's actually on her way?' Blythe said, amazed to have finally found one experienced person to help out.

'Not on her way but here,' a breezy voice declared, and, recognising the voice, Blythe looked up.

'Sue Simpson! What on earth are you doing out here in the back blocks of civilisation?'

Sue greeted her with equal delight.

'Sue Warren it is now. Married a local,' she explained, while Blythe prepared a pre-anaesthetic injection for her patient. 'Three years ago. He was a patient at the Royal and we fell in love. I must admit I was a bit worried about the move from the city, but now I'm here, I love it. I was down home last week. Just got back this morning, or I'd have heard you were here. Don't tell me you've given up your idea of being the top surgeon in Brisbane and come to the bush to help out instead.'

Before Blythe could explain her position was strictly temporary, Cal walked in.

'Sue, what a relief you're here. I thought you'd gone home.'

He greeted the nurse with a quick hug and a far too familiar—in Blythe's eyes—kiss on the cheek.

'I'm back,' she said, 'but later I want to know how you persuaded one of my favourite doctors to come to Creamunna.'

Blythe was checking the patient's chest sounds with a stethoscope but was aware of the byplay. Also aware from the expression on Sue's face of something clicking into place.

'Oh!' Sue said, as if a light had been switched on. 'It's because of—'

Though she had no idea what Sue's revelation was, Blythe was uncomfortably aware of her friend's propensity to blurt out the most embarrassing of suppositions. She cut her short with an abrupt, 'He crashed his plane—that's how he got me here!'

Sue turned to Cal, who said, 'Long story, explain later. Now, have we told this young man what we intend to do?'

Blythe nodded.

'He's signed a consent form,' she said, but must have been looking worried about it for Cal touched her lightly on the arm.

'It's all you can do,' he said. 'Now, let's get him into Theatre. Who's going to volunteer to dress me and scrub my one good hand?'

'I'll do it,' Blythe said, cutting in before he received any other offers. 'I need to talk to you,' she added more quietly, as Sue and another nurse wheeled the patient away.

'I know we're talking exploratory surgery here, and hopefully it will only be a small rupture in a blood vessel causing the problems, but those kinds of things usually seal themselves, and from the distension of his abdomen, there's a lot of blood in there. What if it's his liver? His spleen?'

'We worry about it when you get in there,' Cal told her, moving with such ease with his stick and bound ankle she tended to forget he was injured.

'*We* worry!' Blythe muttered. 'I'm the bit of *we* who'll be doing it.'

'But I'll help—I can talk you through it if necessary. Don't worry, I'm sure the team of Whitworth and Jones would be capable of anything short of a complete heart-lung transplant. And we could probably do that, too, on one of our better days.'

Blythe was so taken aback by this optimism, she glanced towards him to make sure she was walking with the right man.

'Well, I'm glad you're confident,' she said. 'At least that makes one of us.'

Cal's laughter seemed to fill the wide corridor, but then he stopped and his hand on her arm eased her to a standstill beside him. Dark-rimmed grey eyes sought and held hers.

'You're a damn good doctor, Blythe Jones, and I happen to remember you telling me one night that you've done quite a bit of surgery, so I'm confident you're an equally good surgeon. But for some reason you've had your con-fidence knocked about. What you need is a T-shirt that says I'M NOT JUST ADEQUATE, I'M GOOD. OK?'

Cal's eyes compelled her to answer.

'OK,' she said softly, and somewhere deep inside, the frozen chunk of misery that housed her doubts and fears began to thaw.

CHAPTER SEVEN

MIRACULOUSLY, once the operation began, once Blythe started the incision, it was as if she'd never stopped operating. With swift, sure movements, she opened up the skin, separating the layers of muscle beneath it, to expose the abdominal organs—or the dam of blood in which they were bathed.

Sue reacted immediately, using large absorbent swabs to clear the blood, standing close so she could continue to reduce it. Blythe continued to search for the problem, lifting the colon out of the way with warm moist gauze, then shifting the stomach with a large clamp, to reveal the broad ligament connecting the stomach to the spleen. Cutting through that would show her the splenic artery, a large, five-branched vessel that came directly off the aorta.

Instinct and the percentage factor in blunt trauma told Blythe the damage would be to the spleen.

'I'm going to look at the spleen first,' Blythe explained to her team. 'The hoof mark is above the lower ribs in the left upper quadrant, right above the spleen, and Byron mentioned pain in his left shoulder earlier, which suggests referred pain from spleen damage.'

She made a small hole in the ligament, gradually enlarging it as she tied off the small blood vessels that ran through it. Eventually, the dense organ was revealed, blood welling from its upper edge.

'I'm going to tie off the artery,' Blythe said, glancing up at Cal for confirmation. Above the green mask his eyes met hers and the slight nod he gave was more encouragement than agreement.

Encouragement and something else…

Admiration?

Surely not.

But whatever it was, it boosted Blythe's confidence as she passed loops of silk around the artery, tying it off. She looked up at Cal, hoping his monitors would show an immediate improvement in the patient's blood pressure, although she knew instant success wasn't likely.

Cal was frowning at the monitors but he said nothing, so Blythe continued.

With blood draining out of it, but none coming in, the spleen was shrinking in size. The next stage was to cut a larger hole in the ligament, but even with the artery tied off, blood was still seeping into the abdominal cavity.

'Blood pressure dropping. There's still a bleeder in there somewhere, Blythe.'

She turned to the nurse who was acting as runner for the operation, working outside the sterile zone, asking her to set up a second bag of fluid, giving instructions for the rate of flow, but all the time her attention was on her patient as she sought the source of the bleeding.

'Something small, a capillary, would have closed itself off,' she muttered into her mask, 'so it's big. What's close? The renal artery. Please, don't let there be kidney damage as well.'

Anxiety tightened her nerves to the point where her insides quivered, but her hands remained steady as she probed.

'Finish the spleen and then look,' Cal suggested, as time ticked by and Blythe's concern escalated.

She was grateful for the advice. Getting the spleen out of the way made sense, and maybe the blood vessels would seal themselves while she was doing it.

Cutting through the rest of the ligament, Blythe then

drew the spleen a little to the right, to tighten then sever the ligament holding the organ to the left kidney.

Once free, she could lift it out, to clamp and tie off the vein, clamp the artery then check it was completely sealed before cutting the ruptured organ from the blood vessels.

'Neat job,' Cal said, but Blythe knew from his tone they still had problems. Very carefully, she cleaned the remaining blood from the abdominal cavity, and then watched as more collected.

'I haven't got you this far to lose you now,' she told Byron as she searched for the source of the bleeding. Normally a patient could handle a little blood loss, but someone in Byron's fragile state would be at risk, and opening him up again later to find a bleeder would probably kill him.

'Check the splenic artery again,' Cal suggested, and she lifted the tied-off stump of artery. Satisfied the sutures were holding, she was about to set it back down when she realised it was wet with blood.

'It's torn on the other side,' she whispered. 'Above the sutures.'

Relief washed through her as she stitched the tear, swabbed it then waited to see that it remained tightly sealed.

'Got it!' she said to Cal, smiling with triumph, though it was behind her mask so he wouldn't see the smile part.

Then, slowly and carefully, she checked for any other injury the thundering hooves might have caused. It was OK to save the young man's life by removing his spleen, but if she sewed him back up with some other internal injury and lost him through peritonitis, it would all have been in vain.

Once she was satisfied she hadn't missed anything, and Sue was satisfied they hadn't left a swab or clamp behind, she closed him up, put a dressing over the wound and, carefully, straightened her back.

'I'd forgotten that part of surgery,' she said as her muscles protested.

'But not much else,' Cal said, looking at her as if her performance had raised a lot of questions in his mind.

'I told you I'd done a bit of surgery,' she reminded him, then changed the subject. 'How did his lungs handle it?'

'Without an X-ray, we can only go on the lung sounds and oxygen perfusion in his blood, and from those there's no reason to panic yet.'

Cal stepped away from the trolley so the patient could be wheeled into the small recovery room, with Sue watching over him until he regained consciousness.

'Should we X-ray him now we've stopped the bleeding and don't have to keep him flat?' Blythe asked.

He studied her for a moment before answering. She had pulled off her mask and cap and was throwing them in the bin as if she'd done it a thousand times before.

Remembering the skill she'd shown during the operation, he guessed she might have.

Or hundreds of times, at least...

'I know he must feel like your patient, but he should still fly out tomorrow or whenever a plane gets here. And with all kinds of investigative radiology available once he gets to a city hospital, I see no point in putting him through an X-ray here.'

She turned towards him and smiled.

'I agree about the X-ray, but did you think I wanted to keep him? Playing some silly territorial game with that young man's health? We might have stopped the internal haemorrhage but his lungs are the real problem and keeping someone on a ventilator is specialist stuff. Big hospital stuff, with monitors and round-the-clock respiratory techs. Not for the likes of me.'

Cal found himself smiling back. This woman continued to surprise him.

Continued to do other things to him as well, but he wasn't going to think about them. Mind you, it was hard not to when she'd come close and was untying the tapes she'd tied earlier, unravelling him from his theatre garb as casually as she might unwrap a parcel.

Though possibly she'd be excited over a parcel…

This gloomy thought failed to stifle a sudden memory of a previous wrapping scenario—and the memory of fixing safety pins into her curtain dress caused further problems.

She was close enough for him to see the moisture sweat had left on her cheeks, yet he could have been as far away as the moon for all the idea he had of what went on in her head.

Since the night by the fire—and possibly because of it, because she felt she'd talked too much—she'd shied away from any personal conversation, switching subjects so quickly at times it was as if she held up a 'Don't go there' sign towards him.

'I'll stay over at the hospital,' he said, determined to get his mind back on track—a medical track. 'There's usually a bed to spare, and I'll be on hand if Byron's condition deteriorates.'

'You need rest, not a night bouncing in and out of bed to check on a post-op patient,' Blythe said to him, turning away to discard his theatre gear.

'I won't be bouncing anywhere and he's my patient now,' Cal argued. 'I was the anaesthetist, so I'll be in charge of his pain relief. But be sure I'll call you back if there are any problems.'

She turned to look at him, and though he could see tiredness in the bluish shadows under her eyes and the slight slump of her usually straight shoulders, he guessed it was something more than exhaustion worrying her.

'What is it?' he asked, reaching out his good arm so he could rest his hand gently on her shoulder.

She smiled, and half shrugged, though not to rid herself of his touch.

'Let-down, I guess,' she replied, with the honesty he still found both refreshing and surprising. 'Big op—well, big for me—and then that's it.'

Cal felt a surge of empathy so strong he wanted to scoop her into his arms and hold her close. In reality, he'd only have been able to scoop her into one arm, and then he'd probably have fallen over because, though he was managing quite well with his walking stick, that was the hand he used to hold it. And though his ankle was much better, he still needed support.

But the thought was there, so he smiled.

'That's not it at all,' he assured her. 'I've got to check on Byron before I do anything else, but why don't you go through to the doctor's office? I'll send someone in with tea, and whatever leftover goodies Mrs Miller—have you met her? She's the hospital cook—will have baked for staff afternoon tea. We'll have a debrief like a real hospital.'

He was rewarded by her smile, which not only stretched the sensual bottom lip to its full glory but also lit up her dark eyes.

'This place is actually more like a real hospital than some I've been in,' she told him. 'At least the staff here have the time and facilities to treat patients as people, and spend time doing things that make a difference. Offering reassurance, and support for other family members, taking time to talk, to explain what's happening.'

The simple praise—for the hospital, not himself, mind you—flustered Cal so much he muttered something about checking Byron's haematocrit, and hobbled from the room.

* * *

Blythe was waiting in the office when he got back, a tea-tray set with cups and saucers and a plate of scones set on the desk in front of her. She'd broken a scone in half, spread it liberally with jam and cream and had it poised, about fifteen centimetres from her lips, while tears coursed down her cheeks.

'Hey, what's up? What's happened?'

He discarded his stick and propped himself on the desk, touching her shoulder, rubbing at that bit of white skin at the nape of her neck, all the while inwardly cursing his inability to move—to hold her properly.

She responded with a watery grin.

'I think they're happy tears. I mean, they must be, mustn't they? We probably saved that young man's life, taking out his spleen when we did.'

She didn't sound too certain, or particularly happy, and Cal slid his hand around to cup her chin and tilt her head towards him.

'*You* saved his life. All I did was inject the anaesthetic and watch the monitors. And he's doing fine, conscious and responding to questions, though he's still a very sick boy.'

He looked into the soft dark eyes, hoping to emphasise what he was saying. They looked warily back at him—so warily he wondered if he'd done or said something wrong.

Something to upset her...

For some reason, the idea of being the cause of her tears made his gut ache, and he let go of her chin to brush the moisture, very carefully, from her cheeks, then he leant forward and kissed her on that luscious, sexy mouth.

'You were perfect,' he said, straightening up before an urge to linger and explore its infinite softness overcame him.

Well, he'd got rid of the wariness from her eyes, but it had been replaced by astonishment.

'What was that for?' she demanded, so fiercely he was taken aback.

'You were crying. It was a "kiss it better" kiss, nothing more.'

'It had better not have been,' she declared, the brown eyes no longer soft but narrowed and spitting suspicion. 'I might have said some stupid things out there in the bush that night, but I also said I'd crossed you out of contention. And that was even before we became professionally involved. Though I didn't tell you that part of my new approach to men. Definitely no messing about with colleagues. That's rule number one.'

'And rule number two?' Cal queried, teasing her in an effort to cope with his own reaction to the kiss. And his automatic response of disappointment to the 'colleague' statement.

Not that he wanted to get involved with her, of course.

He broke a scone in half and spread it with jam while contemplating these things and awaiting her reply.

'There isn't a rule number two,' she admitted, spooning cream onto his scone before helping herself to more. 'What a stupid conversation, and I'm sorry about the tears. They were for lots of things—but mainly, I suppose, for what might have been. I really wanted to be a surgeon—it's why I did a second year residency and spent most of it on surgical teams. I think I also did more than my share of weekends—the ghastly job of Duty Surgical Officer on call for emergencies like appendicectomies and splenectomies.'

She bit into the scone, smearing cream above her shorter, less full lip, the little moustache so delectable Cal had an urge to lick it off. But if she'd fired up about him kissing her tears away, she'd probably rip his head off if he licked her upper lip.

A pink tongue tip appeared and did the job for him, then she smiled cheerfully and added, 'But I think they were also cleansing tears. Doing that op, for some obscure reason, seems to have wiped away the past once and for all.'

Cal forced his mind away from lovely lips and replayed her explanations in his head. Now he thought about it, her remarks confirmed his suspicion that she'd had the stuffing knocked out of her at some time. Had she failed the first set of exams, which would have put her on track to be a surgeon? But a large percentage of those who sat specialist exams failed the first time, mainly because the pass mark was set so high.

And he knew her well enough to suspect if she'd failed once, she'd have kept trying...

Supposition wasn't taking him too far.

'Why didn't you go on with it? With surgery?'

Blythe set her teacup down and looked up at him, wariness back in the brown eyes. Then she shook her head, making the mass of hair, flattened from the theatre cap, bounce.

'Long and boring story,' she said.

'Not as long and boring as how I came to go into medicine, and you insisted I tell you that. Come on, Blythe Jones, give.'

Blythe studied him for a moment. For a week he'd practised avoidance—oh, he'd been polite enough and had always joined her for meals, but then had scurried away, using work as an excuse. At first she'd been glad as it had given her time to get over the embarrassment of the things she'd said by the campfire, but then his disappearing act had begun to grate on her.

Now, here he was, first firing up her hormones with a kiss that had made her knees vibrate, and now not only spending time with her but prying open bits of her mind she'd clamped shut a long time ago.

'Well?'

She twitched with uneasiness, scowled at him, then muttered, 'It wasn't that important.'

'It was important enough to make you cry,' he reminded her. 'And having seen you in a plane crash, I happen to know you're not the kind who cries easily. Neither do I believe you're a quitter, yet apparently you gave up surgery.'

She couldn't scowl any harder if she tried, and scowling wasn't stopping him anyway. So she sighed instead, then took a deep breath, whittled that heart-wrenching bit of the past down to bare bones and said, 'I was involved with someone also heading towards surgery. We were engaged, living and studying together, then the night before the first exams he happened to mention he didn't think having two specialists in a marriage would work. Listed reasons, mainly to do with stressful occupations and long hours, nights on duty, etcetera.'

Remembering her reaction to that terrible night, she found herself not scowling but smiling.

Viciously...

'Naturally, I asked him if he thought he'd be happy doing something else. I may even have thrown a few things—I definitely threw the engagement ring—but, hell, I'd been the one who'd always wanted to do surgery and I'd been studying my heart out for that exam.'

She paused, blowing out the steam just thinking about that night had generated.

'What I should have done was forget the conversation had ever happened and gone to bed but, no, I packed my gear, went back home and cried all over Mum, and by that time it was nearly morning and I'd had no sleep. I blew the exam, of course, then later I found out he'd been seeing a nurse and the ''two specialists in one family'' story was his cute way of breaking off our engagement so it didn't seem like his fault. Of course, he passed the exam and moved up to registrar, and the thought of having to work on his team any time in the future put me off the idea of trying again.'

She smiled at Cal and shook her head.

'Tacky story, isn't it?'

He didn't smile back, which made Blythe regret telling this tale. What was it about this man that she was always saying things she'd feel embarrassed about later? It wasn't that he was the most chatty of people, inviting confidences because he offered his own so willingly. He was as tight-lipped as an oyster about his personal life—the little she knew she'd had to pry out of him.

Cal watched her stack the cups and saucers neatly back on the tray. Slim, capable fingers moved surely and swiftly, but he knew she was covering whatever emotion telling him this story had generated.

He wanted to say something, but apart from, 'I could kill the bastard who did this to you' he couldn't think of anything that would do. Holding her would have been another option, kissing her an even better one, but now that he understood why she didn't want to get involved with a colleague, neither of those options would be appropriate.

Neither would either of them be a good idea from his viewpoint. He might be attracted to this woman, but in a couple of weeks she'd be gone. In less than a couple of weeks if his shoulder was OK.

So Cal sat and watched her stand up, lift the tray, then walk out of the room, head held defiantly high and the cups on the tray only rattling slightly.

Rattling slightly because she was upset, and he'd caused it by practically forcing her to tell the story?

Good idea or not, he had to follow.

He caught up with her in the kitchen, but evening meals had just been served and the place was a bustle of activity as pots were washed and preparations put in place for the following morning's breakfast.

'I'll check on Byron, then pop home for an hour or so, get some gear so I can spend the night here. I wondered if you'd mind taking off my shoulder bandage while I'm there.' He could begin to exercise his shoulder after a week, and being close to her while she unwrapped him would give him time to make amends.

'Shouldn't you wait until the physio comes later in the week and let her do it and give you exercises?'

Blythe was obviously suspicious, but he knew she was so good a doctor she would be unable not to respond to a medical plea.

'She gave me the exercises—simple stretches, nothing strenuous—last week when she was here. But the sooner I get started the sooner it will be better.' He tried a smile, then reminded her, 'The recommendation is bandaged for a fortnight but gentle exercise after a week.'

'OK, but we could do it here if you like.'

Not exactly a gracious response but he was getting there, though if they stayed at the hospital someone would be sure to come barging in no matter where they sought some privacy.

'At home might be better. While the bandages are off I can have a proper shower, and Mrs Robertson left a lamb casserole for dinner so we could pop that in the oven and it will be ready by the time I'm finished.'

Then, before she could think of any more objections, he added, 'My car's out the front. I won't be long.'

Blythe walked slowly towards the front door. She didn't know what she'd expected him to say when she'd finished the story about David, but she felt he could have managed some response. Now he was acting as if it had never happened—as if she hadn't wrenched open bits of the past and offered them to him on a plate.

Well, to hell with him. That was the last bit of Blythe he'd ever learn about. She'd take a leaf out of his book and make herself scarce at all times when she didn't *have* to be near him.

This would be good from the attraction point of view as well as he obviously wasn't suffering the same chemical surges in his body when he was near her as she was when she was near him.

Even when he'd kissed her, and for a moment it had seemed as if it might go on, he'd drawn away, leaving her uptight—*and* angry about her reaction.

Muttering all this to herself, she waited for him in the car, though she'd cooled down by the time she drove him back to the house. But once inside, the situation deteriorated. She sat him down on a kitchen stool, then stood behind him, thinking that would be better than standing in front, but wherever one stood, unwinding a figure-of-eight bandage from a man's torso necessitated getting close to him.

Close to the ruthlessly cropped hair that twisted as it grew so the back of his tanned neck was decorated with tiny kiss curls.

Kissing kiss curls would be fun...

'I can understand you not wanting to be on that rat's team, but didn't you consider doing surgery somewhere else?'

Cal's question, as she put her arms around his shoulder to roll up the bandage as she unwound it, diverted her from kissing kiss curls.

'Only on a certain part of his anatomy when I found out about the nurse,' she told him, and felt his chest move as he laughed.

She finished unwinding and rerolling the bandages before adding, 'Yes, I did consider it, but I'd no sooner applied for a post in a teaching hospital in Sydney than I got

Ross River Fever and it struck me really badly, probably because I'd been studying hard, and working, and not eating properly. All the things doctors warn people not to do. It took me twelve months to get fully over the debilitating effects, and though I worked part time during that year, I was so far behind by then I knew I wouldn't have the stamina to catch up.'

She was pressing her fingers into his shoulder as she explained then carefully lifting his arm to check range of movement, and though he winced occasionally, he didn't actually complain.

'So London beckoned?'

Blythe let go of his arm and stepped around in front of him to lift his arm towards her and turn it.

'Not London, except as a jumping-off place. I might not have been a qualified specialist surgeon, but I had more surgical experience than a lot of people and I thought with that I might be able to offer something to one of the aid organisations. I was due to join a team going to central Africa when Lileth and Mark announced they were getting married.'

She was talking to distract herself from the impact of being close to him—touching him—the words not nearly as important as the distraction, so she was startled when he pulled away, stood up and positively loomed over her.

'That is so typical of so many people's thinking!' he growled. 'Let's go overseas and do good. Didn't you ever consider the good you could do right here in Australia? Do you have to suffer privation to really feel you're doing good, so living in central Africa is more meaningful than living right here in Creamunna? Do you know how many Australian doctors join aid teams abroad each year?'

He paused to shake his head in frustration.

'I know those people in Third World countries need all the help they can get, but we're importing doctors—hundreds a year—while as many of our own are going off overseas to do their good deeds. Do they never think of doing it in Australia, of spending even a year in a country town like this? That's what I'm trying to do, Blythe. I'm trying to make country service for medical staff at least as attractive as Africa. And it's darned hard.'

'Because it doesn't seem as "good" a deed, if you know what I mean,' she said, feeling out each word. 'And then there's the fear thing. I mean, joining an aid team, you go knowing there are specialists with you. Taking a position in the country, where there's only you? That's scary stuff. If I ever thought about it, which I'm sure I did because there were always recruitment drives going on, I would have assumed I didn't have what it takes to practise in isolation from all the people and equipment available in a city hospital.'

'But these days you're not so isolated. You can lift the phone and talk to a specialist far more easily than you could as a GP in the city, because these guys are there for country doctors. You can get the most recent papers and join discussions on just about anything on the internet, and while we don't have all the latest technological bells and whistles, we have access to specialist services. In fact, the flying surgeon will be here this week. We don't have much to do with him, apart from referring patients. He sees the patients on a previous visit then Sue as Theatre Sister draws up the theatre list. A lot of what he does is basic surgery—hernia repairs, removal of skin cancers, tonsil-lectomies if someone's suffering recurrent infection. You'll meet him Monday—that's tomorrow, isn't it? Bloke called David Ogilvie.'

CHAPTER EIGHT

AFTERWARDS Blythe wondered how she'd avoided passing out on the spot. To hear David's name again so soon after she'd told her pathetic story—and to find he was coming here. Far too many shocks for one woman to handle!

But she'd calmly walked away, telling Cal to do his exercises, heading for the kitchen where she put the casserole in the oven and started peeling potatoes. Her preferred option would have been to head for her bedroom, climb into bed and pull the covers over her head, but Cal might have wondered about that!

Think, brain, think!

But ordering it into action had no effect. Her thinking powers were blotted out by memories of David, and the anguish he had caused her.

She'd leave—get the bus out of town.

No, she'd missed the bus. It had left today at midday and there wasn't another until Wednesday.

Besides, she'd run from David once before. She wouldn't run again.

But she wouldn't go out of her way to meet him either. Why should she? She'd be busy and as the patients he'd be operating on were Cal's anyway, he could handle any consultations necessary.

That was the answer. She needn't see David at all.

Cal moved his arm, stretching the tendons in his shoulder, grimacing at the pain yet at the same time welcoming it as it took his mind off his colleague.

Surely he'd imagined Blythe going pale when he'd mentioned David Ogilvie's name! And her hurried escape to the kitchen was nothing more than her usual habit of keeping things between them on a purely professional level.

Yet something in the air, a sudden tension, told him there was more to Blythe's reaction than he could understand. He just hoped David Ogilvie *wasn't* the man who'd caused such devastation in her life. The man about whom Cal had been harbouring murderous thoughts!

He finished stretching and went through to his bedroom, digging out clean clothes then throwing a toilet bag and his pyjamas into a small bag, ready to take back to the hospital.

He showered, relishing the warm water sluicing over his body after the dusty rodeo, though he wasn't getting much better at shaving left-handed. Then, with the bag and walking stick in one hand and his bandage in the other, he went through to join his visitor in the kitchen. He dropped the bag by the door and held out the bandage to her.

'I hate to be a nuisance, but would you mind wrapping it up again?'

Blythe took the bandage, but try as he may to read something in her expression, he saw only the way her lips pursed slightly as she concentrated, a trick he noticed all too often and which, at times, nearly drove him to distraction.

It was because her lips were so kissable, but for him to be affected by them at times when she was so totally focussed on her job was not good.

She finished, and gave his shoulder a little pat, then she frowned at his bag.

'At the country recruitment talks I attended, most of the jobs on offer were hospital positions. I don't know why I didn't think of it earlier, but shouldn't the hospital here have a medical superintendent? A government-appointed doctor resident at the hospital?'

'Yes,' Cal told her. 'It should. But because there's always been a private practice here—Mark bought the practice from a couple when they retired—finding a doctor for the hospital has never been a priority. We're not even classed as an area of need for doctors recruited from overseas, so if a foreign doctor wanted to work here, he or she wouldn't get special consideration as far as qualifying to work in Australia goes.'

'Because there's already a doctor in the town?' she queried. 'That doesn't seem fair.'

He grinned at her. 'Any more than the scarcity of doctors in Africa is fair?'

Blythe saw the spark of laughter in his eyes and felt her heart judder in her breast. Oh, no, it certainly can't be love, she told herself. She was done with love, and even if she wasn't, Cal most certainly was. The judder must simply have been a different physical reaction to grey eyes rimmed with black, sparkling with laughter at her.

'I'll serve the dinner,' she said quickly, giving herself an excuse to turn away from him.

The phone rang as they sat down, and Cal reached out his good hand to lift the receiver.

Blythe, thinking of Byron, watched him anxiously.

'It's OK—good news, in fact,' he said, putting down the receiver. 'A plane's available to pick Byron up tonight. ETA ten o'clock so we've got an hour. We'll need to go back to the hospital and make sure his notes are up to date, then get him ready for transport. It's an RFDS plane so he'll have a doctor on board for the trip.'

Blythe smiled as the tension drained out of her, but Cal had already turned away, thumbing the buttons on the phone handset then holding it to his ear.

'Merice? Cal Whitworth. We've got an emergency airlift going out tonight. Plane ETA nine o'clock. Will you organise the volunteers?'

There was a pause, then he said thanks and disconnected.

'Volunteers?' Blythe echoed, but if she thought Cal would explain she was disappointed. He simply grinned at her, the mischievous expression causing more movement in her chest as her heart seemed to tug at its moorings.

'You'll see,' he promised. 'Now, eat up. We've got things to do.'

Cal went out to the airfield in the ambulance, with Blythe following in his vehicle. As they reached the outskirts of town and turned onto the main road which passed the airfield a few kilometres out of town, there were a number of other cars on the road. It was almost as if she'd joined a procession.

Wondering where they could all be going at this hour on a Sunday evening—late open-air church service? Full moon revels in some hallowed spot? Was the moon full?— Blythe continued to follow the ambulance. Then it turned off and she realised all the other cars were also heading for the airfield with her.

The ambulance pulled up by a small, corrugated-iron shed, and she stopped beside it and got out, watching in amazement as the cars continued on past the shed.

'What's this?' she asked Cal as he climbed awkwardly out of the ambulance. 'Do the locals have so little excitement in their lives they come out to see a plane land? Is that why you rang someone? To tell her to spread the news?'

Cal smiled at her again, then reached out and turned her around.

'Look,' he said, and she realised the cars were slowing down and seemed to be moving into set positions—some on one side of the runway, some on the other. But their headlights remained on, illuminating the narrow strip of concrete down which the plane would land.

'No lighting in country areas,' Cal explained. 'The locals provide it.'

Blythe shook her head, unable to believe the number of things she took for granted as part of civilised life which simply didn't exist out here in the bush. Yet these people made do. They worked with what they had, and lived rich, full lives.

The sound of an approaching plane made her look up, and she saw the car headlights reflecting off silver wings. Byron's transport had arrived.

Cal handled the transfer of paperwork while Blythe watched the efficient way the patient was moved from one conveyance to another. His parents, who had arrived at the hospital shortly after the operation, were also watching anxiously. They would travel to Brisbane by car and Blythe didn't envy them their thousand-kilometre journey, with worry eating at them every metre of the way.

Yet because emergency air services existed, Byron would be seen by a thoracic specialist tonight—less than twelve hours after his accident.

'There he goes.'

Cal came to stand beside her as the plane took off.

'You could have another trip out here in the morning if you like,' he added. 'Someone brings a car out from the hospital to meet the surgeon and his crew.'

'I don't think I'll bother,' Blythe said, hoping Cal hadn't been able to feel the sudden tensing in her body. 'I remember the back-up of patients we had last Monday, and I think Cheryl told me the first appointment was at eight tomorrow.'

The receptionist had said something like that but, whether the first patient came at eight or not, Blythe had every intention of being in the surgery and staying right there until any risk of seeing David was past.

'Anyway, the patients this fellow will be seeing are your

and Mark's patients, so if anyone needs to liase with him, it should be you. Cheryl can run you over to the hospital.'

Was it tension he could hear in her voice? Cal wondered, as he listened to Blythe list all the reasons she needn't meet the surgeon. Or was he imagining things?

Whatever—it was up to her.

Or so he told himself, trying to ignore a niggle of what must be concern for her, because it couldn't possibly be jealousy.

She drove them home, but without any questions about the bush and medical services in outback areas, which seemed to accompany most of their travelling time. He assumed she usually asked because she knew of his interest in the subject, though sometimes it sounded as if she really wanted to know.

And because he knew that what Creamunna really needed was a husband-and-wife doctoring team, he sometimes allowed himself to believe this and to dream that maybe...

Not that it would be a love match. He was definitely past that, but the physical attraction she'd admitted to wasn't all one-sided, and common interests, a shared profession and physical compatibility should surely be a good basis for marriage.

Cal banged his head gently against the car window. He must be mad to be letting thoughts like that creep in. In another week his shoulder would be out of the restricting bandage, his ankle better, and if he couldn't persuade her to stay until Mark returned, she'd be moving on.

In another week, with two good arms, he could hold her properly...

He banged his head again.

'You OK?'

'Fine!' he lied.

Blythe pulled into the drive and turned off the engine, letting the night quiet settle around them.

'What happened to your plane?'

The question was so unexpected he didn't answer immediately.

'I mean, afterwards,' she added. 'Do you just abandon it out there on Ted's property and buy a new one?'

'I arranged for it to be salvaged—guys go out and pick it up then they and the insurance company decide whether its fixable or if it needs to be replaced. What made you think of it now?'

'The night, the sky, the stars,' she said softly, waving her hand towards the windscreen and beyond it to the velvety, star-bright sky. 'There's a magic about a brightly starlit night that we forget about in the city, I suppose because we never see it.'

And magic in the pearly glow those stars can cast on skin, Cal thought as he watched her watching the stars.

'I'd better get inside,' he said, opening the car door and hustling himself and his stick out before she could come around to offer assistance. 'Haven't checked my emails all day and I've got to email the kids as well.'

Blythe watched him limp away, then slumped back into her seat and closed her eyes. Her mind was such a muddle of emotions she doubted she'd ever sort them out. Her mother had always said to take one day at a time—well, in Blythe's life there was a rip-snorter of a day coming up tomorrow. If she got through it, she'd think about the rest later.

Or not think about the rest—just get her stay in Creamunna over and done with and move on with her life.

But the thought caused an ache where the judder had been earlier, and she knew, some time soon, she'd have to sort through the muddle in her mind.

*   *   *

The next morning went according to plan, as far as Blythe was concerned. She was on her sixth patient when Cheryl phoned to say she was driving Cal to the hospital but would be back shortly, and Helen, the nurse on duty, was manning the desk.

Refusing to think about the man Cal was going to see at the hospital, Blythe concentrated on the forty-five-year-old woman who was 'feeling off', as she put it, and wondered if it might be the beginning of menopause.

'I'm glad you're here,' the patient, Pat Carmichael, confided to Blythe. 'I came to see Mark about it and ended up telling him I was getting headaches because I didn't want to talk to him about it. Not about the personal things that are happening.'

'Tell me the physical symptoms,' Blythe prompted, and Pat listed the discomforts associated with menopause.

'And mentally? Forgetful? Mood swings?' Blythe asked, and Pat chuckled.

'Mood swings sounds so much nicer than temper tantrums, which is how I've been thinking of them,' she said. 'The other day I yelled at my husband for putting dirty clothes in the washing machine when I'd just cleaned it. I mean, where else was the poor man to put his dirty clothes? And hadn't I trained him to put them there, rather than on the bathroom floor, back when we were first married?'

'How did he handle it?'

Pat smiled.

'He put his arm around my shoulders, gave me a kiss, then suggested I come and see you. He said to make the most of it while there was a woman doctor in town, and I think a lot of my friends are doing the same thing. Mark and Cal are both nice guys and excellent doctors, but there are some things a woman feels better about discussing with a woman, aren't there?'

Blythe agreed. She checked Pat's blood pressure, which wasn't high so didn't offer any explanation for sudden temper tantrums, then, knowing Helen was busy on the reception desk, she took a vial of Pat's blood to send away for testing.

'I'll have those results in by the day after tomorrow. Come back and see me then.'

Pat thanked her and departed, but when Blythe's next three patients were all women, she began to think about what Pat had said. Perhaps the appointment of more women to country practice was something for Cal's committee to consider.

Resolving to discuss it with him over lunch, she finished the morning session, only an hour after it should have ended, and crossed the garden to the house, wondering what surprise Mrs Robertson might have prepared for lunch.

It was quiche and salad, but as far as Blythe was concerned it might as well have been dog food. The first person she saw as she walked into the big kitchen area where they ate all their meals was David Ogilvie.

'David told me he was an old friend of yours so I invited him for lunch.'

Cal had risen from the table as she entered the room and moved close enough to rest his left hand in the small of her back, as if ushering her to her chair. Now something in his voice as he made this unremarkable explanation made her look more closely at him.

I'm here for you, his eyes seemed to say, but as he had no idea who David was or how well she might have known him, she must be reading them wrong.

Unless bloody David had been talking!

She glared at her 'old friend', nodded her head and, for Cal and Mrs Robertson's sakes, said, 'David. Good to see you. How are things with you?'

Not holding out her hand to shake his but slipping into the chair Cal held for her, grateful he was there and that the chair had caught her before her knees gave out.

'Great,' David responded, then added fulsomely, 'Even better for having seen you. Though I wouldn't have thought a city girl like you would find much to interest her in a backwater like Creamunna.'

It was like watching a tennis match, Cal thought as his head swivelled to see how Blythe reacted to that remark.

'Ah, but you're not a woman!'

It wasn't anywhere close to what Cal might have expected in an answer, but the smile and wink she threw in his direction as she said it begged him to play along with her, and he was pleased she'd turned to him for support.

'So, you're the flying surgeon,' Blythe continued, when David, obviously put out by her reply, failed to pick up the conversational ball. 'Cal mentioned your name last night. What fun for you, though I don't remember it featuring highly in your plans back when we were studying.'

Cal had felt her tremble as she'd sunk into the chair. The 'we were studying' remark confirmed his guess that this might be the guy who'd let her down. Now, seeing the proud tilt of her chin and hearing the cool politeness in her voice, Cal felt like applauding. But instead he turned to the surgeon, who was smiling—but it was a weak effort.

Had he expected Blythe to fall all over him? Greet him with raptures of delight when he'd ruined her career chances and broken her vulnerable heart?

'Oh, I thought it would be good experience, and I get to see most of Queensland. We cover an enormous area.'

David blathered on, blowing his own trumpet, exaggerating the excitement of what was usually just a series of consultations and operations in different towns on different days. Instead of travelling between major city hospitals, as a lot of surgeons did, he flew between smaller country hospitals.

Cal was tempted to point this out, but Blythe got in first.

'And Joan—was it Joan, the nurse you married? And the baby? I suppose there's more than one now.'

'Jane—her name was Jane and we just had the one child. We're divorced.'

The crisply delivered reply suggested that being married to Jane hadn't brought David much joy, but as the tension in the air was growing by the second Cal wondered if he'd better step in.

He was about to ask David if he saw much of his child when Blythe beat him into speech.

'I suppose you cheated on her, too,' she said calmly, then eased a forkful of quiche into her mouth as if she hadn't just delivered a swordthrust to their luncheon guest's intestines.

'Hey, there's cheating and cheating, Blythe, you know that,' David said, smiling the kind of smarmy smile which had, no doubt, had women falling at his feet for years. But beneath the smile, anger lurked. Blythe's thrust had gone deep. 'And in our relationship, you contributed to the problem. You were so damn focussed on studying for the surgery exams our sex life had virtually stopped. I could never understand how you came to fail, given all the work you did.'

Cal closed his eyes, certain murder would be done, but when he opened them, Blythe was calmly cutting a piece of tomato then settling it neatly onto her fork. She added a sliver of lettuce then lifted it all towards those tempting lips.

'Maybe I didn't want to pass,' she said calmly.

Lips closed around the lettuce and tomato, her mouth moved as she chewed then swallowed.

'Maybe I decided I'd been mistaken in the calibre of

people who went in for surgery. Maybe I decided I'd rather clean out pig swill than be a surgeon.'

She bent her head again and chose a morsel of quiche this time, continuing to eat carefully and calmly, as if David's reply—indeed, David's presence—was of complete indifference to her.

'Lovely lunch, Mrs R., but I've really got to fly. Can you put the rest in the fridge for me for later?'

She pushed away her plate, stood up, eased herself away from the table and said a polite goodbye to David. Then she bent and dropped a kiss on Cal's head.

'See you later, handsome,' she said, and with a little wave of her fingers departed.

'You didn't tell me the two of you were an item,' David said, his tone of voice suggesting this omission was a sin. 'Why I was ever tempted to stray when I was with her, I don't know. I don't have to tell you she was dynamite in—'

'I don't discuss my private life or my friends with anyone,' Cal said, cutting off any further reminiscences. He wondered just how badly the town would miss the flying surgeon if Cal punched him in the mouth and David refused to return to Creamunna in the future.

Cal held his fire—and his fists—then made an excuse of work to do to get away from the man.

'You can take the car back to the hospital and leave it there. Someone will drive it back here later.'

But after David had departed, and Cal replayed the lunchtime conversation in his head, he had to give the points to Blythe.

'Heaven forbid I should ever do anything to deserve your ire,' Cal said, as they sat on the back patio that evening, watching a small flock of rainbow lorikeets play in the water from the garden sprinkler. 'And people say women are the weaker sex!'

Blythe grinned at him.

'I should think you guessed he was the guy I was telling you about—the one I was engaged to. Poor Jane, I feel sorry for her, being caught up with such a loser. I didn't know until later that she was pregnant when he broke it off with me, and do you know what really made me mad? He gave her my ring. The one he'd bought for me—the one I'd chosen!'

She took a sip of her drink, then smiled again.

'But if I'd been her and knew that, I'd have been even more furious. Yes, my sympathies are definitely with Jane.'

'Aren't women's sympathies usually with the woman in cases of men and women falling out?'

Cal had stood up to top up her soft drink, and was standing by her chair when he made this remark.

'Certainly not,' Blythe told him, looking up so she could see his face. 'Every time I think about you and Grace, my heart practically bursts with pity for you. I know you made it sound as if she and Chris couldn't help what happened but, whether they fell in love deliberately or not, nothing would have made it easier for you.'

Cal smiled at her and brushed his hand across her hair.

'Don't let your soft heart ache for me, Blythe,' he said. 'I got over all of that a long time ago, and now I find I love my new life, and I look forward to the challenges ahead. There's so much I can do out here, whereas at home, back at Mount Spec, it was only going to be more of the same for ever. Oh, I would have introduced new blood lines into the cattle herd, looked into breeding programmes, stuff like that, but it would only have been building up the company's wealth and assets, whereas here, and with the rural medicine committee, I feel I'm achieving something worthwhile.'

He laughed at himself, adding, 'Will you listen to that garbage? You'd think I see myself as the new Albert Schweitzer. I don't, of course, but I might be able to make a small difference.'

Blythe believed he'd make more than a small difference—he was that kind of man—but if he thought he'd diverted her from personal matters, he was mistaken.

'You say you're over it all, yet you're determined not to marry again,' she reminded him. 'Doesn't fit, Dr Whitworth.'

'You're one to talk,' he retorted. 'One bad relationship with a sleazeball, and you're going for loveless sex from now on.'

'OK, so we're both wimps,' she conceded, then she remembered what she'd wanted to talk to him about, and changed the subject, mentioning Pat and the number of other women patients she was seeing.

'I know,' Cal said. 'I was thinking the same thing myself only yesterday. The ideal situation for practices like this is a married couple medical team. Can you think of incentives we could offer that might entice young married couples—or even older married couples—to come to the country to practise?'

'Transport would be a start,' Blythe said. 'You know how people who work for the government and bigger international companies and are sent overseas get a free trip home once or twice a year. Or they can use their trip to fly family members to visit them. Could you finance air fares from places where there are airline services? Maybe charter trips for people in places like Creamunna? Charters are expensive and cheap air fares don't exist in country areas, so if the government, or a private agency, provided funding for travel, that would be one less cost the couple

would have to bear. I think fares for the kids to travel to
and from boarding school as well—that kind of thing.'

'It's a good idea and I'll follow up on it,' Cal said, but
though he'd listened to Blythe's suggestion and knew it
was a good one, the major part of his mind was stuck in
another groove. Back in the 'marrying Blythe for the good
of the community' groove it had jolted into the previous
evening.

Marrying Blythe wouldn't hurt his sex life any either,
and he suspected it was that option which was deepening
the groove.

He was wondering what she'd say if he suggested it to
her when Mrs Robertson called them in for dinner, but the
thought remained lodged in his brain, so it was almost
inevitable it would eventually escape.

They were up to dessert, a sticky banana pudding and
ice cream, and he was going demented watching her spoon
food into that mouth. Had Grace's eating habits ever attracted his attention?

Had he had to watch every spoonful slip between her
lips?

'If *we* were married, we'd be a husband and wife medical team, and with an outside income I can afford air fares
to the city any time you wanted to go. I don't suppose
you'd like to marry me.'

That stopped the movement of the spoon halfway to the
lips.

'To ensure Creamunna has two doctors? I don't think
so.'

Blythe shook her head and the spoon continued its journey, but when she'd finished the mouthful she didn't immediately begin work on the next selection. Instead, she
looked at him, and an almost imperceptible wrinkle of a
frown creased the smooth skin of her forehead.

'And aren't you kind of jumping the gun here? You

won't need another doctor if Mark comes back. I'd be redundant.'

Oh, I doubt you'd ever be that, Cal wanted to say, but realised that was his mind in the other groove again.

'Besides, *you* don't want to marry again, remember, and I wouldn't like to be cast in the role of sacrificial lamb if you're making the decision purely for the good of the community. I'd be an obligation and you'd grow to hate me within months—and hate the community too, most likely, for forcing you into the situation.'

She waggled her thankfully empty spoon at him.

'You should think these things through more carefully before blurting them out. A man could get into trouble that way. I can think of a dozen women, including a couple of nurses at the hospital who sigh as you limp by, who'd say yes so quickly you'd be at the altar before you knew which way was up.'

Blythe put the spoon back down in the bowl, her appetite completely gone. She thought she'd handled the astonishing conversation remarkably well, considering it was the second bout of evasive verbal action she'd had to take in one day.

When Cal had first mentioned marriage, the juddering had started again—in fact, her heart had flopped around in her chest like a just landed fish in the bottom of a dinghy. But though she talked big about no-strings-attached sex, there was a bit of her, tucked deep inside where dreams dwelt, that knew marriage, for her, would have to be the real thing. She'd want love, and Cal certainly wasn't offering love.

And she'd want to have her loved one's children, and he'd already pushed 'family' into the BTDT basket.

She sighed, then looked up to find him watching her, the grey eyes narrowed as if he was trying to peer into her skull.

'That was some sigh,' he said. 'Want to talk about it?'

'I was thinking, if I keep eating Mrs R.'s desserts, I'll have to book two adjacent seats on the bus when I eventually leave town. I'll be too big to fit into one.'

CHAPTER NINE

BLYTHE tossed restlessly in her bed.

She should be used to it by now! She'd been tossing around this way for ten days. Although her flippant remark about putting on weight had effectively ended Cal's strange conversation the previous Monday, the ridiculous idea kept surfacing. Especially as he now seemed to be going out of his way to be pleasant to her. He appeared in the kitchen while she was having breakfast, ate lunch with her and had joined her in front of the television in the evenings. Even, a couple of nights, suggesting they take a walk after dinner.

But she hadn't fallen for that. If eating breakfast with a charming Cal Whitworth put her equilibrium in jeopardy, being out under the stars with him was like diving into a pool full of sharks!

She knew he'd only put the ridiculous proposition to her—and was probably on this 'be nice' campaign—because of his determination to provide better rural medical services, so that wasn't a worry.

It was her own behaviour keeping her awake and tossing, night after night.

First the judder, then the heart-wrenching exercise, then linking words like 'love' and 'marriage' in her mind and feeling excited about them. This was not the behaviour of the new-woman, sexually liberated Blythe.

OK, so she hadn't done much about putting her ideas into action but, then, she hadn't really been attracted to anyone with whom she'd wish to trial them.

Until she'd met Cal...

No, it was useless speculating about Cal. Cal was out, both as a sexual adventure type of partner and a permanent one. The first because he was practically related, in a step kind of way, and also because she suspected she wouldn't stay unemotionally involved—or should that be emotionally uninvolved?—and the second option was a no-go because the marriage he wanted was a different animal to the one she might eventually consider.

But ruling Cal out of contention didn't stop her remembering that Sunday evening's kiss, or how it had burned against her lips, making her feel deliciously hot and cold at the same time.

Just thinking about it made her feel hot without the cold right now, and in the end she gave up trying to sleep and walked out through the French doors onto the veranda that ran along the front and around both sides of the house, with access from all the bedrooms.

She leant against the railing and looked up at the sky— at the myriad stars that never failed to fascinate her. She'd miss the night sky when she returned to the city. Though there'd be plenty of stars in the sky in Africa…

Blythe shook her head. Conjuring up images of Africa no longer worked any magic. Maybe she could find another outback town—apply for a hospital position somewhere in the outback, or join a country practice…

'Would you like something to help you sleep? A glass of warm milk? Mild sedative? You've had a couple of big days.'

Cal's voice was so quiet it seemed to fit right into the night, not startling her at all.

'No, I'm fine, just couldn't sleep,' she said, turning from her contemplation of the sky to watch him approach.

He stopped beside her, close but not touching.

'You're not using your stick,' she said, and though she couldn't see his face clearly, she sensed he was smiling.

'No, I thought it would get in the way.'

Then, before she had time to register the meaning of this cryptic comment, he put his hand on her shoulder and leaned forward, brushing his lips across hers so gently it might have been a fragment of the breeze that sighed softly through the bushes.

But the breeze turned into a cyclone as he pressed closer, the kiss now demanding a response.

Aware of his injury, but tired of fighting the attraction, Blythe slid her arm around his back and met his kiss with a fervour she couldn't remember ever feeling before. He tasted of toothpaste, clean and cool, though the tongue that teased between her lips was hot and searching, forcing her to meet and match its exploration.

As the intensity of the kiss deepened, Blythe felt her nipples tighten. She pressed closer, wanting to ease the tightness yet knowing it wouldn't go away so easily. Blood throbbed through her veins, warming hidden places deep within her and making her skin tingle with desire.

All this from a kiss?

Her mind struggled to make sense of it, and reminded her this was not a good idea. It suggested Cal was doing this to prove his point about the attraction between them, and she should be backing off. But her body wanted to cling to Cal's and her lips had no intention of losing contact with his.

He's injured, she reminded herself, but her hands knew this, avoiding where she might give pain and sliding up instead to press against the crisply cut hair, holding his head both to steady herself and to keep his mouth right where she wanted it.

But he wasn't playing fair, moving his lips from her mouth, pressing them against her temple, then teasing his tongue towards her ear.

'No ears,' she managed to murmur. 'Drives me nuts.'

'I'd love to drive you nuts.'

It sounded like a threat—of the very nicest kind—or maybe a promise, but Blythe's mind was so busy cataloguing sensations she hadn't felt for a long time, she couldn't waste time sorting threats from promises.

'Maybe tie you to a bed with soft silk ropes and nibble on your ear until you begged for mercy.'

His mouth was travelling south as he suggested this scenario, travelling to where the fine cotton nightdress she'd bought at Mrs Warburton's was proving a very inadequate barrier to seeking, probing lips.

'Such creamy skin—it drove me wild from the start,' he murmured, and while Blythe bleated things about his shoulder, and this not being a very good idea, his tongue found her nipple, already rigid with excitement, and teased around it, firing heat and longing that speared down through her body to pool between her thighs.

So what if he was nearly related, she decided. She'd handle christening-type embarrassment when it happened. The way she was feeling now, a little embarrassment would be a small price to pay...

'You might not want to marry me, but would it hurt to give in to the attraction?' His lips had found their way back to hers, and they asked the question she'd already answered in her head.

But there was another question.

'Your shoulder...'

'It's OK. It doesn't hurt when it's wrapped up and we'll improvise.'

Cal made it sound as if improvisation would be sexy and delicious fun, and more excitement heated Blythe's skin yet brought goose-bumps out on her arms.

Still kissing her, he manoeuvred the two of them towards his bedroom, part of the house she'd never entered.

Or thought to...

And improvise they did, for so long, and so thoroughly, Blythe was surprised to find herself able to function the following day.

She'd woken in Cal's bed, having eventually slept so deeply she hadn't heard him leave it. He'd left her a note, explaining Mrs Robertson had driven him to the hospital so he could check the post-op patients.

Which had also removed Mrs Robertson from the house so Blythe could scuttle back to her own room.

She showered and dressed for work, then met up with the housekeeper in the kitchen.

'You're both up late today,' Mrs R. remarked. 'Cal was barely out of bed when I arrived.'

'I think it's all this country air.' Blythe crossed her fingers behind her back as she said it, although this was more a fib than an outright lie.

She fixed herself a bowl of cereal, then stirred the spoon around in it, not wanting to eat in case the anxiety gnawing at her stomach rejected the option of food.

She carried it out to the patio, knowing she was late and should be hurrying but caught in the quicksand of morning-after doubts. Being outside didn't alter the fact that unless she left town immediately, sooner or later she'd have to face Cal.

Just thinking about the previous night made her skin heat, so how was she going to react to seeing him in daylight—greeting him—talking…

Behave as if nothing had happened?

Which was OK as long as she didn't let her hormones loose. They'd be sure to want to do a bit of smoochy-coochy touching stuff, which, any fool could tell, would not be Cal's scene at all.

It wasn't really hers either, so why was she even thinking such a thing? Smoochy-coochying would probably make her more nauseous than the spoonful of cereal she'd just forced down.

No, Cal had made it clear he was giving in to attraction when he'd first kissed her last night, and while it might have led to mutually satisfying—hell, it had been fantastic—sex, that's all it had been.

Perhaps she could take her cue from him. See how he behaved and follow suit.

Yeah?

This was a man who, in all the time she'd known him, had never shown any emotion. He would certainly do 'cool' far better than she could ever hope to.

Blythe scraped the cereal into a pot plant, then had to pull leaves across the soggy flakes to cover the mess.

A mess, that's what this Cal situation was.

So forget it and go to work.

She sighed, but obeyed this sensible direction. Well, she might not have totally forgotten the problem, but she did hurry across to the surgery, where she was pleased to find the first appointment was even later than she was.

It was a typical GP's morning, syringing out a child's ear, doing a postnatal check on a new mother then spending an enjoyable few minutes cooing over the six-week-old infant, checking an elderly man's blood pressure and ordering blood tests to see if the vitamin B injections he was on were helping his anaemia—a mixed bag of patients, but all of them warmly appreciative of whatever she could do for them.

Would marrying Cal be so bad? she found herself wondering as she took a break between patients to drink the coffee Cheryl had brought in.

Forget Cal, phone Brisbane to see how Byron is. You haven't checked for days!

She did just that and was pleased to hear he was off the

ventilator now, and would probably be released within days.

Blythe was sure the coffee tasted better once she knew that. She set the empty cup aside and reached for the next file.

Helen knocked then poked her head around the door.

'Carly Anstead's next. She's a bad asthmatic and comes in for a new script for Ventolin. Mark's been keeping an eye on her weight as well.'

She seemed about to say more, but a teenager who had to be Carly was right behind her, and she waved the girl in then shut the door.

Blythe introduced herself.

'I know you must get sick of this every time you need a new prescription, but I've got to check you out—listen to your lungs, take your blood pressure, check your lung capacity.'

'I know,' Carly grouched ungraciously. 'You do all this stuff but it doesn't make me better.'

'You're right.' Blythe was prepared to sympathise, but she was suddenly aware of undercurrents in the air between herself and her patient. Carly was displaying a wariness so strong it verged on paranoia.

'And I don't need weighing to make my asthma better,' she snapped, confirming the vibes Blythe had been getting.

She bent her head, reading Mark's notes, seeing the words 'eating disorder' and a string of question marks after them. The recent weights were there as well, dropping steadily.

Blythe stood up, handed Carly the peak-flow meter to measure the volume of expired air the girl could blow out.

The result wasn't bad, considering the asthmatic problem, and her chest sounded reasonably clear.

Blythe talked to her about her medication—when she used the Ventolin, how often she had acute attacks that needed drugs administered through a nebuliser to ease the constriction. Carly answered easily, but when Blythe mentioned school, and how she handled attacks when she was there, the girl closed up again.

'I don't want everyone at school thinking I'm a freak,' she snapped, when Blythe persisted.

'So you don't use your Ventolin even when you need it?'

Carly answered with a scowl.

'I know of a young person who died of an asthma attack on a school bus,' Blythe told her. 'Not because she was being silly, like you are when you don't take medication, but because when she pulled her puffer out of her school bag, some kid grabbed it, just to tease her, and threw it to one of his mates, who continued the game. The bus driver didn't realise what was happening, though he knew the kids were messing about and he yelled at them to stop. By the time anyone realised the girl was seriously ill, it was too late.'

Blythe let the story hang in the air while she wrote out a new script for Carly.

'I know sometimes, especially when you're young, you have times when you think being dead might be better than being alive, but it really isn't. It's a cold, lonely place, and there's no changing your mind once you're there. Whereas while you're alive, even if life seems to suck for a while, you know there's always a chance it will get better. Maybe not straight away, but eventually.'

She pushed the script across the desk to the young teenager.

'Sometimes talking about things that are bothering you helps. I know there are some things you can't talk about to your mother, and even to your friends, but there's usually someone around. Doctors are good, or nurses at the hospital, or maybe a teacher you really like—even a primary teacher you liked when she taught you years ago.'

She busied herself again, jotting notes in Carly's file.

'I'll be here for another little while and if you don't want to talk to me at an appointment, phone me at home—the doctor's house number is in the phone book—and we could meet somewhere, or go for a drive.'

She closed the file then looked up and smiled at Carly. 'OK?'

Carly nodded, and Blythe could see the tears that had filled her eyes.

'Now's OK, too,' she said, coming around from behind her desk and kneeling beside the girl so she could put her arm around her shoulders. 'If you want to talk now, we can.'

Carly pressed her head against Blythe's shoulder and sniffed.

'I don't want to be dead,' she whimpered, then, as if ashamed of saying even that much, she moved away, standing up and hurrying from the room.

Blythe thought about following her out, then decided that wouldn't be a good idea. Forcing Carly to talk about her problems would be counter-productive. The girl had to be ready to share them with someone for there to be any hope of solving them.

Helen came in again as Blythe was still staring at the door.

'Kid problems all over the place,' Helen said. 'Cal just phoned to say his daughter Jenny is in trouble at school. His brother is flying down from the territory, and will collect Cal at the airport and they'll both go on to Brisbane to see the girl.'

'Jenny's in trouble? Blythe felt her heart stutter to a standstill, then resume beating with rapid, uneven strokes. 'She's only a kid. What kind of trouble?'

Helen shrugged.

'No idea, but Cal's not leaving until two. He said he'd see you at lunch.'

At least with his mind focussed on his daughter I won't need to worry about the 'morning after' scenario, Blythe told herself, but it didn't make her feel any better. In fact, thinking about Cal worrying made her feel nauseous again. True, she hadn't seen much of his children at the wedding, but she'd seen enough to make her realise he loved them dearly, and the way he talked about them—the way he phoned and emailed them—underlined his closeness.

With an effort she forced her mind off Cal—for the second time today—to concentrate on work.

'Is it serious, Jenny's trouble?'

Cal was in the kitchen, grim-faced and pale, when she walked in after surgery. A small travel bag was parked beside the back door.

'Only in that she doesn't want to stay at school, but, damn it all, she has to board. There's really no alternative.'

He put the plate of sandwiches Mrs Robertson had left for their lunch on the table, then rubbed his neck as if thinking about his daughter was causing physical pain.

Though her fingers itched to touch him, Blythe resisted, concentrating on the conversation, not the memories of the previous night which just seeing him had brought back in vivid Technicolor. Accompanied by the urge for just a little smoochy-coochy stuff.

'No alternative?' she echoed. Surely there was always an alternative if one thought long and hard enough?

'Well, this year she could continue School of the Air,' Cal admitted. 'But there's only a few weeks of term left, so why not stay put? Then she starts high school next year, and though School of the Air caters for high school students, the supervision is much harder and Grace just isn't prepared to take it on. Neither will she accept a new governess for Jenny, even if I pay for one.'

'So the poor kid will be forced to stay in an environment she hates,' Blythe said. 'And you've got to be the bunny to tell her that?'

'Don't you start,' Cal snapped at her. 'You don't understand the first thing about it.'

At least that killed off any chance of smoochy-coochy!

'No, I don't!' Blythe snapped right back at him. 'If I did I might be able to see why Jenny can't live with you during term time and go to school here.'

'Oh, for heaven's sake, it would be impossible,' Cal told her, scowling ferociously now. 'I'm on call at least every second day, and if Mark decides to leave, I could be called out at any time and she'd be left on her own.'

'Mrs Robertson is here during the day and Mark might decide not to leave,' Blythe told him, and was rewarded with another scowl.

'So who made you the expert on childcare?'

'You don't need to be an expert to know that forcing Jenny to stay on where she's unhappy will only lead to trouble. So, rather than go down to see her with only one thought in mind—to tell her she has no options—why don't you start thinking laterally? Consider what alternatives there might be. Think about why she's unhappy— why she doesn't want to stay. For heaven's sake, Cal, she's what, twelve? How much trouble could she be if you brought her home with you—at least until the holidays? I've agreed to stay until Mark gets back. I'll do the calls, and you can spend some time with your daughter.'

The tension on Cal's face lightened slightly, then a strange look came into his eyes. A look that told her he, too, was thinking of the previous night.

'But—'

He reached out, as if to touch her, and Blythe backed hurriedly away.

'But nothing!' she said firmly. 'You and I are going nowhere, we both know that, and your daughter's future is far more important than the pair of us satisfying a bit of lustful attraction.'

'So that's all it was,' he said, his voice tight and strained.

'It's really all it can be, isn't it?' Blythe replied, while sadness gripped her heart and squeezed until it felt every drop of blood had been drained out of it.

The grey eyes which so mesmerised her scanned her face, asking questions—seeking answers...

'I've brought the car to the bottom of the back steps so you can put your case in the back,' Mrs R. announced as she came through the back door, efficiency personified. 'I'll drive you out to the airport because Blythe will have to get back to work,' she added.

'Thanks,' Cal said, bending to lift his small bag. He straightened up then turned back towards Blythe. 'Well, I have to go.'

'I know,' Blythe said, then the hormones she'd been restraining broke loose, demanding at least a little smooch. She crossed the room and touched him lightly on the shoulder, while her hand ached to grip and hold him, to shake him and tell him she loved him...

Which would be a nice burden to land on his shoulders when he was totally preoccupied with a rebellious daughter.

'Take care,' she said instead, and she kissed him swiftly on the cheek.

Cal hesitated, looking down at her, his eyes once again searching for something, then he shook his head, and she knew it was all over.

CHAPTER TEN

CAL loaded his case into Chris's plane, wishing he could deposit the load of confusion he was carrying as easily.

'Have you any idea what's behind this business with Jenny?' he asked as he climbed in beside Chris. 'I wish I'd had more time to talk to her at the wedding.'

'I doubt she'd have said anything. It seems we're all against her—you, me, Grace. Especially Grace as far as I can make out, though she's done everything for those kids.'

The roughness in his brother's voice told Cal Chris was as worried as he was. Chris had always loved the kids and Cal knew he'd been a good influence on them, fathering them on a day-to-day basis without ever usurping Cal's position in their lives.

'We'll sort it out,' he said, touching his brother lightly on the shoulder.

Chris turned and smiled at him.

'United against the world?' he said, reminding Cal of the slogan they'd used when they'd first gone away to boarding school.

Later, when they'd lost their parents, it had become even more important to them.

'United against the world,' Cal agreed, feeling more at ease with his brother than he had since Chris and Grace had fallen in love.

'So how *is* your world?' Chris asked, and Cal looked out at the endless blue sky through which they flew.

'Kind of muddled at the moment,' he admitted. 'To be

honest, I can't think past the next few days and sorting out what's wrong with Jenny.'

'But generally—medicine and all?' Chris persisted. 'Are you happy with that part of things? You know there's more than enough work for the two of us at Mount Spec if you ever change your mind and wanted to come back. Or Grace and I could move to one of the other properties. I've always fancied living in the Kimberleys, so now we've bought Warrendock over there, I'd be happy to go.'

Cal shook his head.

'I've been out of it too long now, Chris, so even if I did want to return, which I don't, you'd have to stay in charge. Though, I went out to see a patient on Buralong recently. Now, there's a great property, not far from Creamunna, and it's been on the market for a while. It's only twenty thousand hectares but the river runs through it so it's well watered even in times of drought. It'd make a top-class fattening property. You could truck young steers down from Mount Spec...'

They talked cattle for the rest of the journey, though Cal kept thinking about the low-set, gracious house on Buralong and the manager's house for someone who'd do the day-to-day running of the place while he continued practising. From the moment he'd seen the place, he'd known it was what he wanted, to combine the two loves of his life—medicine and cattle.

Two loves? his head queried, while images of a tall, blonde-haired woman moving through the airy rooms at Buralong danced in his head.

He should phone Blythe when they reached Brisbane.

And say what?

Sorry to love you and leave you?

Thanks for a memorable night?

Are you sure you don't want to marry me?

He hauled back his wandering thoughts. At least he

could phone and apologise for the way he'd spoken to her. He'd had no right to take out his own confusion on Blythe, but seeing her there in the kitchen and remembering…

He rested his head back against the seat and closed his eyes, but vivid images of the night before flashed across the back of his eyelids, so he had to open them again.

Marriage? Why on earth did he keep thinking of marriage? He'd tried that once and it had proved disastrous, yet his thoughts kept tripping over the damn word. He'd even blurted it out to Blythe at one stage.

Suggested she marry him as a solution to the medical problems in Creamunna.

Which it would be—so marriage as a contract, like a work contract—

'Jenny home, which isn't really an option. We haven't told anyone yet, but Grace is pregnant and she's not very well.'

Chris's voice brought Cal out of his speculation with a jolt.

He looked at his brother, saw a pale wash of embarrassment, mixed with a huge amount of absurd pride, on his face.

'But, Chris, that's wonderful! I'd wondered—thought maybe you and Grace didn't want children of your own. You're happy?'

Chris beamed at him.

'Don't I look it? Grace says I'm like a cat with two tails.'

Then the glow faded.

'Though she's really been quite sick. I've been very worried about her.'

'She was always sick right through her pregnancies,' Cal told him. 'Some women are.'

But now the news was sinking in, he wondered if perhaps Jenny suspected. If that was why she was unhappy.

Another child in a family changed all the dynamics. Jenny had been the 'baby' for a long time…

Perhaps he *could* bring her back to Creamunna. Just till Christmas—spend some time with her…

Jenny would be his prime concern—and sorting out her problems should keep his mind off Blythe!

Blythe went back to work and was just about to leave when Carly phoned. Sensing any delay might put the girl off talking, Blythe arranged to pick her up.

'Is there somewhere, perhaps a little way out of town, where we can talk?' she asked, as Carly climbed into the car.

'Out by the river would be nice,' she replied, directing Blythe to a small park where fat grey gums leaned towards the murky, green-brown waters of the local river. They sat on the bank, throwing stones in the water, watching them disappear. The only things marking their passing were the ripples moving back towards the shore.

Blythe listened to the young girl who felt her asthma made her different—who'd stopped eating, hiding food in her pockets at mealtimes and later throwing it away— thinking being thin would make her popular enough for boys to forget she suffered from asthma.

Knowing the problem wasn't going to go away immediately, Blythe let her talk, then later, as she drove Carly home, she suggested they meet again before too long. But as she headed back to the doctor's house, she realised that Mark would be back in a few weeks, and her job in Creamunna would be finished.

Would she have time to do anything effective to help Carly, and even if she did, would the girl slide back into bad habits without Blythe's support?

Depression settled on her shoulders like a pair of large

black crows, cawing misery and regret in her ears, mocking her...

Depression?

Black crows?

What had happened to the new woman?

She poured herself a glass of cold lemonade and took it onto the veranda where she considered the crows—seeking to identify them.

One was easy—how she felt about Cal and the fact that the relationship between them, such as it was, was doomed. Maybe the crow was laughing!

Crow Two was more surprising but, no matter how she tried to skirt around the issue, it came back to the fact that her time in Creamunna would be over when Mark returned and, believe it or not, *she did not want to go.*

Admittedly, her feelings for Cal were mixed in with that reluctance, but beyond that, she was enjoying her work—enjoying practising medicine in the outback. London and Africa had lost their appeal. The red soil plains, with their clumps of spinifex and grey-green saltbush scrub, were now more beautiful to her than city streets, the banks of the murky river where she and Carly had talked more attractive than a sandy beach.

But beyond the physical impact of her new surroundings, the local people had captured her heart. The laconic, dry-humoured cattlemen who treated their ailments and injuries as nothing more than minor inconveniences—the cheerful, busy women of the town who delivered meals-on-wheels, worked at the charity shop, volunteered on several committees, cared for their menfolk and kids, yet still found time to do exquisite embroidery, or paint, or work with clay or silver.

Country towns had a lot going for them.

The phone summoned her out of this introspection, and she walked back into the empty, echoing house.

'I just wanted to tell you I've taken your advice. Jenny's coming home with me. We'll be back tomorrow afternoon. Could you ask Mrs R. to make up a bed for her?'

Heart aflutter at just hearing Cal's voice, Blythe told herself to settle down and make some appropriate response.

'Yes.'

Dreadful, but the best she could manage right now.

'Yes? That's all? No I told you so?'

The warmth in the words told her he was teasing, but its effect on her nerves made her snappy.

'I didn't *tell* you anything,' she reminded him. 'Whatever I might have said would only have been a suggestion. After all, what do I know about child-rearing?'

'Did I say that to you? I'm sorry. I was worried.'

He paused, but Blythe was so taken aback by the apology she couldn't fill the silence.

'Confused as well,' Cal added. 'It wasn't the best timing in the world, was it?'

The new woman tried valiantly to pull herself together.

'Things happen,' she said, hoping she sounded more offhand than she felt. 'Anyway, I'll tell Mrs R. about Jenny coming. Any other messages?'

'No, I guess not.' The warmth had gone and his deep voice sounded curiously flat—though it would, considering it was coming to her across a thousand kilometres of countryside. 'I'll see you tomorrow, then.'

Blythe replaced the receiver and stood looking at the phone. Tomorrow. Cal would be back tomorrow.

With his daughter...

Jenny seemed to accept Blythe's presence in the house in the same way she accepted Mrs Robertson but, having known the older woman from previous visits, she was far friendlier to her than to Blythe.

Cal, on the other hand, was increasingly edgy and irritable. Not with Jenny, but with everyone else, so eventually both Helen and Cheryl commented on it. When Blythe's friend, Sue, meeting her for a coffee after work, also mentioned how short-tempered he was, Blythe decided she'd better do something about it.

'I want to talk to you some time today,' she told him when he'd been back five days and, though he'd reverted to avoiding her as much as possible, he'd happened to walk through the kitchen while she'd been eating breakfast. 'Not now, because I've a pile of path tests I want to check before the first patient, and not here, because there's always someone else around, but perhaps at lunchtime. At the surgery. Will you be around?'

'Where else would I be?' he growled, indicating his right arm which was still in a sling. 'You know the X-ray showed the break's not healed so even though I've got the bandage off I still have the damn sling. I should be seeing patients one-handed. I can't take this doing nothing.'

'You haven't exactly been doing nothing,' Blythe reminded him. 'You've been getting to know your daughter again, and seeing the patients at the hospital. You've been doing the outpatient sessions over there with a nurse to help you. That's more than most people with a broken collarbone would do.'

'Getting to know my daughter? Jenny's bug-eyed in front of the television all day and hushes me if I try to talk to her. As for doing a ward round—there've been eight to ten patients max this week and all I've done in Outpatients is tend the occasional cut or scrape. Meanwhile you're working yourself ragged trying to do two doctors' work, and don't say you're not, because I can see how peaky you've become.'

'Peaky? Me peaky? As if!'

Blythe held out her arms and spun around so he could see all of her still ample body.

But Cal was obviously not impressed.

'It's your face. It looks thinner.'

You're looking at my face? Noticing how I look? Blythe knew the spurt of joy she felt was totally inappropriate, especially for a liberated woman, but before the joy could even take hold, another thought squelched it. She finished her cereal and rinsed her bowl under the tap. If Cal could look at her closely enough to think her face had grown thinner, then he couldn't be experiencing the rampant longings that filled Blythe's body every time she so much as glanced his way.

She was getting through the days by seeing as little as possible of Cal. Even when they were together for the evening meal, she'd perfected the art of looking only at the tip of his right ear, and then for the shortest possible period of time because ears inevitably reminded her of *that* night.

Realising she hadn't responded to his remark—well, not verbally—she turned back, but before she had time to focus on the ear tip, Jenny called to him and he walked away.

'So, why the summons? Do you want to leave? Had enough of the country life?'

Blythe looked at him—right at him this time—and shook her head. He'd stalked—which was impressive, given he was still hobbling slightly—into the office, pulled out the patient chair, and slumped into it, arms folded belligerently across his chest.

'That's why I wanted to talk to you,' she told him, coming around the desk and propping herself against it so she could point at his arms and glare down at him. 'That attitude you're carting about with you like a bad odour. It's wearing thin, buddy boy. Cheryl's sick of it, Helen's sick of it, and even the nurses at the hospital are complaining. OK, so everyone's prepared to cut you some slack because you're injured, but you can't be in much pain now. Yet since you returned from Brisbane you've been like the proverbial bear with the sore head. What's got into you, Cal? Why are you so grouchy?'

He stared at her for a moment, then sighed. He even had the hide to smile!

'It's not a laughing matter,' Blythe warned him—damn, she shouldn't have been looking right at him when he'd smiled!

'Oh, I'm not laughing,' he assured her, standing up so he was suddenly very, very close. 'But tell me, are you not the slightest bit perturbed by this situation? Not in the least aggravated? Frustrated? Infuriated because we can't go back to where we were before? Can't explore more options—possibilities?'

He was so close now she could see the tiny patches where his left-handed shaving had missed a bit of beard hair—so close she could smell the musky maleness of him.

Too close! She slid away, pretending she needed to pace to absorb what he'd just said.

'You're talking about sex?' she demanded, while her heart jittered and her thighs burned with memories. 'You're cranky as all get-out because we can't keep having sex? It's not your injury frustrations you're taking out on the staff but your sexual frustrations? That's teenage stuff, Cal Whitworth.'

He'd taken up her position now, propped against the desk, arms folded again, but protectively this time.

'That's how I feel,' he admitted. 'Like some half-witted teenager, filled with lust and longings.'

He shrugged broad shoulders.

'Stupid, isn't it? Here I am, supposed to be solving

Jenny's teenage problems and I've reverted back to some-one little older than she is.'

Huge sigh, then he unfolded his arms and rubbed his free hand across his face.

'Not that I'll ever solve Jenny's problems. She won't talk to me. All she says is she hates boarding school, full stop.'

'Have you stopped to think that might be all it is?'

Cal frowned at her.

'But everyone thinks they hate school—especially boarding school—at some stage of their life. It doesn't mean the child should just give up. That isn't how things work.'

Blythe looked at him and smiled, though there seemed to be more sadness than joy in the expression.

'No, it's not, is it?'

She studied him for a moment, or maybe she was study-ing something on the wall beyond his right ear. He turned to see what was there—a muscle chart!

'But Jenny's not the problem as far as your attitude is concerned. You are. Are you going to tone things down? Revert to being Dr Nice Guy?'

'I suppose I'll have to,' Cal conceded. Actually, until Blythe had brought it up, he hadn't realised he'd been letting his feelings show. At least, not that badly.

'Thanks for pulling me up on it.'

She'd stopped pacing, halting beside the glass-fronted cabinet where Mark kept his reference books.

'No worries,' she said, but her voice was so tight and strained he stared at her, seeing more tension in her shoul-ders and in the arms crossed tightly across her chest.

'This is bloody stupid!' he growled, closing the distance between them with one long stride. 'Look at you—you're as tightly wound as I am.'

He touched her shoulder.

'Tell me you don't feel fire run along your nerves whenever we're together. Tell me your blood doesn't pulse faster, your heart rate rise, when we accidentally touch. Tell me that doesn't happen, and I won't ravish you with kisses right here and now, Blythe Jones.'

He didn't give her time to tell him anything, swinging her around and drawing her close against his body, then denying any hope of words with a kiss that carried all his longings and frustration.

But it was her response that really sent him over the edge—the fervour of her kiss, the demands of her tongue, the tremble in her body as she pressed against him.

'Blythe.'

Her name was no more than a suggestion on his lips, then they were moving towards the examination table, fumbling with clothes, finding contact with each other's skin and giving in to the demands of their bodies.

'I can't believe we just did that,' Blythe whispered, not much later. She was sitting on the edge of the table but her head was slumped against Cal's chest. 'What if Helen or Cheryl had come in? Worse, what if Mrs R. had sent Jenny over to find out why we weren't at lunch?'

She moved away, her hands scrabbling to rearrange her clothes. Helpful as ever, she then reached out to help his one-handed effort with his trousers.

Cal felt he should stop her—or move away—or say or do *something*! But his mind had seized up. He'd never been a man who'd let his libido rule his brain—in fact, the very opposite, missing out on any amount of offered sex because his brain was firmly in control.

Until a tall, shapely blonde had made him wrap her in a curtain, and his sex drive had been going haywire ever since.

'This can't keep happening,' the blonde now announced.

She'd moved to a position of safety behind the desk and Cal had the oddest notion that if she could have moved further away, perhaps crouched behind Mark's skeleton, she would have.

'No.'

Good, she looked startled. Did she think he was going to suggest it became a daily ritual?

'It's a most uncomfortable way to conduct an affair and, as you said, Jenny could have walked in.'

The thought made him feel icily cold.

'I didn't mean *this* can't keep happening, as in a quickie in the office, but the whole thing can't,' Blythe said. 'We're not having an affair. I'm not into affairs, especially not with colleagues.'

Cal wondered about arguing that he wasn't much of a colleague at the moment, then realised that wasn't the crux of the matter.

'But I thought that's what you were into. Casual sex.'

He watched colour climb into her cheeks.

'Yes, well, maybe that's what I thought I might *get* into, but what we just did, that's casual sex, isn't it? And now I've tried it, I don't think I'm going to take to it. But an affair is more than that—it's more than casual—and I don't want that either.'

'What *do* you want, Blythe?'

Cal couldn't believe he'd asked that question. He knew damn well what a woman like Blythe would want. No matter how hard she might deny it to herself, she was made to be a wife and mother. He could picture blonde-haired moppets clustered around her feet, pudgy hands clinging to her skirt.

Then he thought of Grace, pregnant again, and the ice returned to his veins.

If Jenny's trouble stemmed from a sense of injustice that her mother was having another baby, how much worse would the poor girl feel if her father started breeding again?

His mind had wandered so far that when a whispered 'I don't know, Cal' hit his ears, he had no idea what Blythe meant.

He wanted to leave—to get away so he could attempt to sort through his thoughts—but he couldn't just walk away.

Not without saying something!

But what to say?

'Come on, we're late for lunch.'

The look she shot him out of heavy-lidded brown eyes told him he could have done better, but he knew that himself. He opened the door and walked out, assuming she'd follow.

Blythe stared at where he'd been. Now he was gone, she realised she was hungry, but there was no way she was going up to the house and putting herself in Cal's proximity again so soon. Her skin still tingled from their quick but, oh, so satisfying love-making, and her mind had taken leave of absence so blankness filled her skull.

She walked out through the deserted reception room and raided the biscuit tin in the tearoom, munching on something very bland while she tried to get her brain working again.

'Blythe? Are you still here?'

Jenny's voice, calling from outside. With a burst of gratitude Blythe realised Helen and Cheryl had, as they always did, locked the outer doors when they'd left for lunch. Cal would have used his key to come in, but Jenny had been safe from witnessing their uninhibited behaviour.

'I'm coming,' she called, and walked back out to let Jenny in through the main entrance. 'Hi. You want an appointment? Professional visit? Or is it social?'

Jenny had been polite to her, but had never sought her

out, so Blythe was intrigued enough to be able to put aside what she and the youngster's father had just been up to.

'Sort of social and sort of professional,' Jenny told her with a shy smile that made her look more like her father.

Cal shy?

Blythe shook her head to get him away.

'You know you were telling Dad about the girl called Carly, and talking to her out by the river. I wondered...'

She hesitated, and Blythe stayed very still, knowing Jen could tip either way right now.

'Wondered if you'd take me out there. To see the river. Maybe talk.'

Grey eyes with dark rims looked helplessly at her.

'Of course. When? This afternoon? I finish at three because there's evening surgery. Would that suit you?'

Jenny nodded then, to Blythe's surprise, she spread her arms and gave Blythe a quick hug.

'Thanks!' she said, and turned away, then looked back to say, 'You won't tell Dad?'

Blythe smiled at her.

'No way! It's a girl thing. I only told your dad a bit about Carly because I'll be leaving here soon and I wanted him to keep an eye on her. Maybe find someone else for her to talk to.'

Jenny gave a satisfied nod and trotted off, long, gazelle-like legs taking her in swift strides back to the house.

CHAPTER ELEVEN

THEY drove out to the river in an awkward silence. From time to time Blythe pointed to something—swimming pool, skateboard park—and Jenny nodded and peered dutifully through the car window at whatever was indicated.

Then they pulled into the small park and stopped in the shade. Blythe turned off the engine and looked at Jenny.

'We can sit here or on the grass by the river. Carly and I sat out there.'

Jenny opened the car door and led the way.

'The river's so dirty,' she said when Blythe joined her. 'I wouldn't like to swim in it. We can swim in the river at Mount Spec but Chris won't let us because of crocodiles.'

Blythe shuddered at the thought.

'I don't blame him,' she said, and Jenny laughed.

'Dad doesn't understand about school,' she said, picking up a stick and breaking it into little pieces. 'He says there are times in life when we *have* to do things we don't want to do, and that's that.'

'Well, there are,' Blythe said, careful not to cast Cal as the baddie. 'But there are times when it's right to *not* do things we don't want to do. That's especially true when we're growing up and other kids might want us to, say, smoke a cigarette or try a drug. Then you definitely don't have to do something you don't want to do.'

'It's kind of like that at school,' Jenny said, piling the broken bits of stick on a rock and choosing another one to break. 'Not cigarettes or drugs, of course, it's far too strict for that kind of stuff, but there are these girls who are kind of leaders. Everyone wants to be their friend, and I was, but they think it's nerdy to study for exams and to do well, and I want to be a doctor like Dad when I grow up and so I have to do well in exams, but when you're nerdy they tease you.'

The explanation came out in such a rush it took a few seconds for Blythe to take it all in.

'Aren't there other girls who like to study? Who want to do well? Couldn't you be friends with the nerdy girls?'

The look of horror on Jenny's face was enough answer.

'Oh, no!' she said. 'That would be way too gross! Besides, the nerdy girls are all day girls.'

Blythe understood the distinction. Being a boarder didn't stop you being friends with day girls but you had less out-of-school time to get to know them, so generally the boarders stuck together.

Jenny continued to talk, the conversation giving Blythe further insights. Though a number of the boarders were girls like Jenny, from outback properties, and another group were from Asian countries, the rest—Jenny's friends—were from wealthy local families, the girls boarding either because they were in trouble at home and their parents thought the stricter confines of boarding school might sort them out, or because their parents travelled a lot and it was easier to have the girls board full time.

'Poor kids!' Blythe said, and Jenny agreed.

'I know,' she said, with a maturity beyond her years. 'At least I know Mum and Dad and Chris have sent me there because it's best for me, not to get rid of me, but it's awful, Blythe, it really, really is.'

She began to cry, sniffling miserably into a scrunched-up handkerchief she produced from the pocket of her shorts.

'Hey, we'll work it out,' Blythe told her, putting her arm around the thin shoulders and drawing the slim body closer. 'For a start, we can find out about the local high school here. I know your dad worries that you'd be on your own too much if you stay with him to go to school, but if you think you'd like to stay I'm sure he could organise something.'

Blythe thought for a moment, then added, 'I don't suppose Sam hates school as much as you do. If he did, he could come and live with his father too, and the two of you would be OK on your own if Cal was called out.'

Jenny laughed.

'Poor Dad!' she said. 'He doesn't know what to do with one kid at his place— he'd never manage two. He really should have got married again and had more kids so he learned about them. And he wouldn't have been so lonely then either. And probably not so crabby. And it would be neat, having babies in the family.'

Blythe, niggled by the thought of Cal being married, was about to point out—coolly—that babies grew up when Jenny continued.

'But what you said—about Sam—well, he absolutely loves boarding school. He loves being with other boys and fighting and pushing each other and playing rugby. It's different for him because he'll go home to work at Mount Spec when he finishes so he doesn't need to be a nerd.'

'No,' Blythe said, understanding that this made all the difference.

She thought about things for a while, then said, 'If you want to do medicine, you will need a really high score in your final year of high school, then you'll have a three-year degree course at university—most people do science for pre-med—then a four-year medical course. It's a long haul, Jenny.'

The dark head nodded vigorously.

'I know that,' she said, 'but it's what I really, really want to do.'

'Well, it's up to your father, of course, but even if he agrees to you staying here to go to high school, you might find a country high school can't offer you the subjects you need in your last two years to get the score you want. You might have to go to boarding school then.'

Mutiny tightened the girl's lips, but then she relaxed.

'That's three years away and if it happens, I could go to some other boarding school, couldn't I?'

'I suppose so,' Blythe said. She felt exhausted, drained by the worry she'd felt all afternoon since Jenny had asked to speak to her.

'Great!' Jenny announced, standing up and heading back towards the car. 'So, you'll talk to Dad?'

'I'll talk to your father? I thought you didn't want me to tell him! And why me?' Blythe spluttered, scrambling to her feet and following the girl. 'You managed to tell me all of this, why can't you tell him? Believe me, he'd far rather hear it from you than from me.'

Jenny turned towards her and the eerily familiar grey eyes looked directly into hers.

'I've tried to tell him, but it's like he's got a block somewhere and the words just won't go around it. I talked to Mrs R. about it and she said you'd be able to explain it all, and that he listens to you.'

She grinned at Blythe.

'Mrs R. said it would be the best thing in the world if he married you. I don't suppose you'd like to marry him, would you?'

'I'm not going to dignify that question with an answer,' Blythe said, and swept around the back of the car, spoiling the effect slightly by tripping over a stick on the way.

Like to marry him? Of course she'd like to marry him! Marrying him would be like—well, she couldn't think what it would be like, but...

She jabbed the keys into the ignition, switched on the engine and backed out of the park.

Common sense intervened. Marry him? When she'd known the man—was it less than a month?

And probably fell in love with him that night by the fire when he'd insisted on holding her and had told her stories of the bush...

Love! What rubbish!

That was common sense again, scoffing and reminding her about David and what happened when love went sour.

'Can we drive past the high school? Would you come with me to have a look over it if Dad agrees? With him, too, of course, but you'd know better if it was OK. It's a long time since Dad went to school.'

Blythe found herself agreeing—after all, it was a harmless enough request.

Then she realised the implications. Visiting the school would come after Cal agreed—if he did—which would come after she herself talked to him—if she did...

They arrived back at the house and she parked the car.

'You will do it—talk to him?' Jenny pleaded, and Blythe sighed.

'I've got evening surgery tonight,' she reminded the young girl, 'and there won't be time before that.'

'Afterwards?'

A vague memory of her own teenage years—of pestering her mother, going on and on like water dripping on stone—came back to Blythe and she knew Jenny would keep asking until she got the answer she wanted.

'OK,' Blythe told her, though the very last thing she wanted was a tête-à-tête with Cal. She'd do it in the kitchen, where there was a lot of light.

*   *   *

He was sitting on the veranda—where there was no light at all apart from the dangerous kind supplied by moon and stars—when Blythe returned from the surgery.

'Can I talk to you?' she said. She didn't realise until he responded with 'Wow, twice in one day!' that she'd said the same thing earlier.

Remembering what had happened at the last 'talk' made her blush, but she continued resolutely past him.

'In the kitchen,' she said, and expected him to follow. But it was Jenny who entered, from the living room, where the music blasting from the television reminded Blythe that there was more to having a teenager in the house than she'd considered.

'Where's Dad?' Jenny whispered. 'Are you going to talk to him now?'

'Yes, I am,' Blythe told her, her aggravation with the situation adding just a little acid to the words.

'You might be better doing it on the veranda,' Jenny suggested. 'I've got the TV going in here.'

'Oh, really?' Blythe said, but as Jenny picked up a packet of chocolate biscuits and headed back towards the noise, Blythe realised sarcasm was wasted on the young.

She walked reluctantly back to the veranda.

'I thought once you heard the noise in there you'd decide out here was better,' Cal said, and she could have belted him across the head for being so smug.

Then a wave of exhaustion—more emotional than physical—washed over her and she sank down into one of the comfortable canvas chairs and lifted her legs to rest them against one of the long arms provided for that purpose.

'Tired?'

Cal's voice was seductively soft.

'I guess so,' Blythe said, huffing out a sigh. 'Jenny wanted me to talk to you.'

As soon as the words were out of her mouth she realised

she'd said the wrong thing, but it was too late to suck them back in because Cal had already taken exception to them.

'Jenny asked you to talk to me? Why, may I ask? I've flown to Brisbane, I've brought her back—against my better judgement, I might add—I've taken her around with me, sat and watched television with her, tried to work out what's upsetting her, with very little help from the young madam, now she's appointed you as a go-between. I'm her *father*, for heaven's sake! Why can't she talk to *me*!'

Blythe heard pain behind the anger, and because of that she bit back the angry response that sprang to her lips, breathed deeply—then once more when that didn't work—and finally answered.

'Perhaps because you *are* her father,' she said gently. 'Because of that, more than anything in the world, she wants to please you. And for that reason she's stayed all year at a school she hates.'

'That's ridiculous. If she hated it from the beginning, why didn't she say something? She was here in the Easter break and I saw her at the wedding. When I asked her about school, it was fine!'

Blythe dropped her feet back down and pushed her chair closer to his, knowing he was hurting and wanting to touch him—though touching him was as risky as running barefoot through a bushfire...

'She managed, and it probably was fine, but I imagine things came to a head with end-of-year exams,' she said, resting her hand on his arm. 'Apparently she's a clever girl, your Jenny, and she likes to study, but the group she was in with—the trendy girls—think studying's for the birds and they tease the kids who want to do well in exams.'

She felt rather than saw Cal turn towards her.

'Is this something to do with nerds?' he demanded. 'She said something about not wanting to be a nerd and I told her that was stupid. You have to be your own person, and do what you want to do, no matter what other people think.'

Blythe sighed again.

'That's OK when you're older,' she said, 'but at Jenny's age, standing out in any way is anathema. If the in group had pink and purple spots, she'd want them, too. It's natural. And quite apart from not wanting to stand out, there's the fact that kids of that age can be cruel to anyone they perceive to be different.'

'But the school has an excellent scholastic record. There must be clever girls there she can befriend.'

Cal knew this was important, but he was missing something here—was it secret women's business? Stuff men would never understand?

What he did understand were the sensations Blythe's hand, resting innocently on his arm, was causing.

'The clever girls are either day girls or Asian boarders who, no doubt because of language, have their own group. I'm sure in time Jenny would fit in there, but is it really necessary, Cal? Is there no way you could keep her here?'

'I could if I was married,' he said, then straightened in his chair and turned to Blythe, clasping the hand that rested on his arm. 'But that's the answer. If you married me it would solve all our problems. There'd always be someone at home for Jenny, and even if Mark doesn't leave, we could share the work at the practice.'

He was about to list other advantages, not least of which was a satisfactory sex life, when she pulled her hand away, stood up and said, 'Go boil your head.' And walked away.

Not the most encouraging of replies, he realised, but she was tired. Frustration with his temporary disability ground within him, but there was nothing he could do about it right now, any more than he could follow Blythe to her room right now, so he set it aside and went back through the conversation to the bits about Jenny.

Surely that was something he *could* fix.

Blythe was up early. She'd have breakfast and go across to the surgery and hide out down there because the one thing she knew for sure and certain was that she couldn't face Cal right now.

So finding him in the kitchen when she tiptoed in to grab some cereal was a setback.

'What are you doing up so early?' she demanded.

'Getting you some breakfast,' he said, so calmly she peered suspiciously at him. He was beating eggs in a bowl, awkwardly left-handed but getting the job done. And now she'd woken up a bit more, she could smell bacon grilling. 'I thought it would give us a chance to talk.'

'Huh!' Blythe muttered. 'As if we haven't done enough of that, though you weren't so keen yesterday.'

'I know,' he said, sounding suspiciously penitent. 'But I talked to Jenny later last night and she really does want to come and live here.'

He tipped the eggs into a pan before continuing.

'Actually, the more I thought about it, the better it seemed.'

He gave a huge grin that weakened Blythe's knees so she had to grip the back of a chair to remain upright.

'I'm pleased to think she'd want to live with me, but more pleased for myself, Blythe. I hadn't thought about it before, but it's as if someone's given me a special present—a share in a few years of my child's life. That's what I wanted to talk to you about. Obviously, if Mark decides to stay in Creamunna, I won't stay on in this house. I've kind of known that all along, and now, with Jenny, it's definitely out of the question. I've seen a house—well, a property out of town but with a great house on it—and if I shift out there and get a housekeeper—'

'You won't need a wife.'

Blythe wasn't sure where *that* had come from, but she couldn't stop the words popping out.

Cal looked startled, as if he'd forgotten ever bringing up the marriage idea.

'Well, no,' he said, stirring the eggs. 'I wouldn't *need* one, but I might still want one.'

'And what am I supposed to make of that?' Blythe demanded, talking to his back as he turned to drop bread into the toaster.

'Whatever you like,' he said cheerfully. 'After being told to go boil my head last time I proposed to you, I'm not about to do it again.'

Disappointment squirmed through Blythe's intestines, but this teasing, almost light-hearted mood was a side of Cal she'd never seen before and she had no idea what he was thinking.

Or where she stood...

If anywhere!

He walked across to the table and set down a plate with crisp bacon and soft scrambled eggs.

'Eat!' he ordered. 'Big day ahead. I told Jenny we'd go out and look at the house when you finish work. We'd both like you to come.'

Blythe dropped into a chair and looked at the food he'd set in front of her.

'I didn't know you could cook,' she mumbled, pushing egg onto a fork, then realising she wasn't the least bit hungry.

'There's a lot you don't know about me,' he said, putting a pot of coffee on the table and slipping into the chair opposite hers.

'And a lot you don't know about me,' Blythe reminded

him, becoming aggravated by the overwhelming good cheer. 'Which hasn't stopped you making ridiculous proposals.'

'Ridiculous? I thought they were practical.' Grey eyes gleamed with laughter, and to avoid them Blythe looked back down at her breakfast.

She cut a piece of bacon and shoved her fork through it. 'Oh, they were that all right,' she snapped. 'Marry you to help the practice—marry you to babysit Jenny.'

'Ah!'

She was jamming the bacon into her mouth so couldn't immediately respond, but once it was chewed and swallowed, she glared at him.

'And what's that supposed to mean?' She paused then read the innocent expression on his face and forestalled his next comment. 'And don't ask what's what supposed to mean. That "ah" you said—that's what.'

Now he grinned, and tiny little butterflies started flitting around inside her chest, making breathing difficult.

'I was wondering what might make you agree—to marry at all, not necessarily me. The way you talked about David, I thought a practical arrangement might appeal to you, but I must have been wrong. So, tell me, Blythe Jones, what kind of proposal would you accept?'

He was teasing her and she knew it, but the stress of the last few weeks had worn her down to the stage where she could no longer deny what she was feeling.

She put down her knife and fork and looked directly at him.

'A proposal that involved love,' she said. 'A proposal that was more a commitment to caring and sharing than a contract of any kind. I know I talked big about not getting involved, but I've realised I'm not that kind of person, Cal. I need to be involved—with my work, with the people I care about. I need to love and be loved in return, to give myself wholeheartedly to whatever I take on. Marrying you for the practice, or for Jenny's sake, would be a halfway thing and I don't think I'm a halfway kind of person.'

He stood up and came around the table, resting his good hand on her shoulder.

'I don't think you are either,' he said quietly. 'I think you're the most wholehearted person I've ever met—throwing herself into whatever's happening with total commitment.'

Now he's going to walk away, Blythe thought, staring down at congealing scrambled eggs through a mist of tears, while her heart broke in two.

But he didn't, though he moved, pulling out the chair beside her and dropping into it.

'Look at me,' he ordered, and she sniffed and turned towards him, intending to focus on the tip of his right ear.

'No, right at me, Blythe, because this is important. This is so important I might not be able to get it right, but I need to try.'

Cal lifted his hand and brushed one finger across her cheek, then lifted the gleaming tear to his lips and sucked it off.

'Heaven forbid I should ever make you cry, my love,' he said gently. 'Or hurt you in any way…' He drew in a deep breath before continuing, 'Because hurting you would hurt me—would devastate me. You came into my life—a tetchy, snippy woman with an attitude problem. But you made me laugh and then you stayed, helping me out, and you poked and prodded at my defences, which, I might add, have taken years to build up, until I didn't know whether to murder you or marry you. Having to live with you didn't help either. Here was this incredibly sexy woman, in the same house but not in the same bed.'

He took Blythe's hand and lifted it to his lips, kissing each finger in turn.

'Except for that one exceptional night!'

His eyes gleamed with memories, and Blythe held her breath, wanting to hear more yet still uncertain where Cal might be going with this.

'I'd denied love for so long, I didn't recognise it when it came along, so of course I made every mistake in the book.'

Now he took both her hands and kissed each palm in turn.

'But even an idiot catches on eventually.'

He looked directly at her, his expression wary.

'I love you, Blythe, and I can't see that ever changing because the more I get to know of you the more there is to love.'

His smile was kind of tortured as he added, 'Is that good enough? Would you marry me for love?'

Blythe hesitated then leaned towards him and kissed him on the lips, then snuggled her head against his chest— carefully!

'So I won't have to work in the practice, or be there for Jenny or do any of the other stuff you might want from a wife?' she teased, and felt his arm tighten around her back.

'Some of the other stuff I might want from a wife would be fun, don't you think?' he whispered, sending flares of desire through her blood. 'And I can just see you *not* being there for Jenny—as if you could help yourself!'

He eased her away from his body so he could look into her face.

'That's what I love about you—the way you care. The way you go that extra yard to help—whether it's an injured pilot out in the bush, or a schoolgirl who needs a friendly ear. Jenny's blessed and so am I—that's if you're actually going to say yes.'

She saw his uncertainty and for a moment considered

teasing him, but she'd be teasing herself as well, so she answered him.

'Yes,' she said, then smiled. 'Third time lucky, eh?'

'Forever lucky, now you're going to be mine,' Cal said, his voice husky with the love that shone in his eyes.

Modern Romance™
...seduction and
passion guaranteed

Tender Romance™
...love affairs that
last a lifetime

Medical Romance™
...medical drama
on the pulse

Historical Romance™
...rich, vivid and
passionate

Sensual Romance™
...sassy, sexy and
seductive

Blaze Romance™
...the temperature's
rising

27 new titles every month.

Live the emotion

MILLS & BOON®

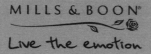

MILLS & BOON®

Live the emotion

Medical Romance™

OUTBACK ENCOUNTER *by Meredith Webber*

As a research scientist, Dr Caitlin O'Shea's usual problem is not being taken seriously – her stunning blonde looks get in the way! But she's not expecting her work in tiny Outback town Turalla to have so many other challenges – like Connor Clarke, the town's overworked doctor…

THE NURSE'S RESCUE *by Alison Roberts*

Paramedic Joe Barrington was determined not to give in to his attraction for nurse Jessica McPhail – he just couldn't get involved with a mother, and Jessica had to put her child Ricky first. But when Joe risked his life to rescue Ricky, he and Jessica realised that the bond between them was growing stronger by the day.

A VERY SINGLE MIDWIFE *by Fiona McArthur*

Beautiful midwife Bella Wilson has recently regained her independence – and she doesn't want obstetrician Scott Rainford confusing things. Twelve years ago their relationship ended painfully, and she won't let him hurt her all over again. But now, working side by side, they find their feelings for each other are as strong as ever…

On sale 6th February 2004

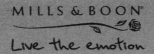

Behind the Red Doors

Sassy, sensual...and provocatively playful!

Vicki Lewis Thompson

Stephanie Bond

Leslie Kelly

On sale 6th February 2004

Available at most branches of WHSmith, Tesco, Martins, Borders, Eason, Sainsbury's and all good paperback bookshops.

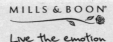

MILLS & BOON®

Live the emotion

PENNINGTON

BOOK EIGHT

Available from 6th February 2004

*Available at most branches of WHSmith, Tesco, Martins, Borders,
Eason, Sainsbury's and most good paperback bookshops.*

PENN/RTL/8

4 FREE

books and a surprise gift!

We would like to take this opportunity to thank you for reading this Mills & Boon® book by offering you the chance to take FOUR more specially selected titles from the Medical Romance™ series absolutely FREE! We're also making this offer to introduce you to the benefits of the Reader Service™—

- ★ FREE home delivery
- ★ FREE gifts and competitions
- ★ FREE monthly Newsletter
- ★ Exclusive Reader Service offers
- ★ Books available before they're in the shops

Accepting these FREE books and gift places you under no obligation to buy, you may cancel at any time, even after receiving your free shipment. Simply complete your details below and return the entire page to the address below. *You don't even need a stamp!*

YES! Please send me 4 free Medical Romance books and a surprise gift. I understand that unless you hear from me, I will receive 6 superb new titles every month for just £2.60 each, postage and packing free. I am under no obligation to purchase any books and may cancel my subscription at any time. The free books and gift will be mine to keep in any case.

M4ZED

Ms/Mrs/Miss/Mr ....Initials.....................................
BLOCK CAPITALS PLEASE

Surname ....

Address ....

....

....Postcode....................................

Send this whole page to:
UK: FREEPOST CN81, Croydon, CR9 3WZ
EIRE: PO Box 4546, Kilcock, County Kildare (stamp required)